PLAYING THE GAME

A YORK BOMBERS HOCKEY NOVEL, BOOK 1

LISA B. KAMPS

Playing the Game Copyright © 2017 Elizabeth Belbot Kamps

All rights reserved.

Except for use in any review, the reproduction or utilization of this work in whole or in part in any form by any electronic, mechanical or other means, now known or hereafter invented, including xerography, photocopying and recording, or in any information storage or retrieval system, is forbidden without the express written permission of the author.

The York Bombers is a fictional semi-professional ice hockey team, its name and logo created for the sole use of the author.

All characters in this book have no existence outside the imagination of the author and have no relation to anyone bearing the same name or names, living or dead. This book is a work of fiction and any resemblance to any individual, place, business, or event is purely coincidental.

Photographer: CJC Photography
http://www.cjc-photography.com

Cover Model: Josh Voto
www.Instagram.com/whoisjoshvoto

Artwork and Cover Design by Jay Aheer of Simply Defined Art
http://www.simplydefinedart.com/

Formatting by Rêverie Design & Formatting
www.foreverie.co

All rights reserved.

For Michele Polich, who first introduced me to hockey all those years ago!

CONTENTS

Prologue	1
Chapter One	5
Chapter two	11
Chapter Three	18
Chapter Four	26
Chapter Five	32
Chapter Six	37
Chapter Seven	46
Chapter Eight	55
Chapter Nine	64
Chapter Ten	72
Chapter Eleven	76
Chapter Twelve	87
Chapter Thirteen	94
Chapter Fourteen	101
Chapter Fifteen	110
Chapter Sixteen	118

Chapter Seventeen	124
Chapter Eighteen	133
Chapter Nineteen	144
Chapter Twenty	153
Chapter Twenty-One	161
Chapter Twenty-Two	172
Chapter Twenty-Three	185
Chapter Twenty-Four	192
Chapter Twenty-Five	200
Epilogue	204
Book 2: Playing To Win	209
About the Author	211

Other titles by this author:

THE BALTIMORE BANNERS
Crossing the Line, Book 1
Game Over, Book 2
Blue Ribbon Summer, Book 3
Body Check, Book 4
Break Away, Book 5
Playmaker, A Baltimore Banners Intermission Novella
Delay of Game, Book 6
Shoot Out, Book 7
The Baltimore Banners: 1st Period Trilogy
Books 1-3 Boxed set
The Baltimore Banners: 2nd Period Trilogy
Books 4-6 Boxed set
On Thin Ice, Book 8
Coach's Challenge, A Baltimore Banners Intermission Novella
One-Timer, Book 9
Face Off, Book 10

FIREHOUSE FOURTEEN
Once Burned, Book 1
Playing With Fire, Book 2
Breaking Protocol, Book 3
Into the Flames, Book 4
Second Alarm, Book 5
Coming Soon

STAND-ALONE TITLES
Emeralds and Gold: A Treasury of Irish Short Stories *(anthology)*
Finding Dr. Right
Time To Heal
Dangerous Passion

THE YORK BOMBERS
(a brand new hockey series, hitting the ice in February, 2017)
Playing The Game, Book 1
Playing To Win, Book 2
Playing For Keeps, Book 3

Be sure to sign up for Lisa's newsletter, *Kamps' Korner*, for exciting news, sneak peeks, exclusive content, and fun, games, and giveaways! You don't want to miss it!

Can't wait for the newsletter? Need to get your fix of hockey, firefighters, passion and news daily? Then please join Lisa and a great group of readers and fans at *Kamps Korner on Facebook*!

PROLOGUE

Hands, small and smooth, trailed across his body. Delicate, almost hesitant. His skin burned wherever they touched. Only his tightly-reined control kept his body from arching, kept him from reaching, seeking.

He held himself still, only his chest moving with each harsh gasp of air that shuddered through him. But fuck, he wanted to touch her. *Needed* to touch her. To feel the softness of her skin, the dampness of her flesh under his own.

"Don't move." Her whispered words were more of a command than a plea. Harland sucked in another breath and dug his hands into the mattress. A brief spurt of thankfulness shot through him that it wasn't a cheap mattress, in a cheap motel that rented rooms by the hour.

Or worse, in the backseat of the beat-up junker he was embarrassed to call his own.

They were back at his house, behind the locked door of his stuffy room. The late afternoon sun streaked through the cracked blinds, adding to the heat that settled around them. But it was more than the heat of the midsummer afternoon. It was the heat of *them*, of their bodies twisted together, slick skin against slick skin.

He had planned for this day for too long. Planned? Hell, he'd *wished* for this day. Dreamt about it. Fantasized about it.

The fantasy didn't come close to the reality.

He knew how precious the gift was that she was giving him, knew what it would cost her. And he wished he could give her more. So much more. She deserved wine and roses and diamonds and candlelight—things he didn't have to give her. One day, though, when he made it big. She'd have all of that and more.

But for now, there were no flowers. No fluffy mattress and satin sheets or soft music. He did have candlelight, though. A pair of crappy dusty pillar candles he'd found shoved in the back of a cabinet that were supposed to smell like vanilla and spice but smelled more like musty wax, which was better than the scent of old hamburger grease and stale cigarettes that permeated the small house where he lived.

It didn't matter, though. Nothing mattered except the two of them, their naked bodies entwined together, flesh firm and soft and slick.

And her touch. God, her touch. Had he imagined it like this? No, not even close. And when her trembling hand finally closed around him, her touch soft and sweet and gentle and shy, he nearly lost it.

Harland clenched his jaw and tilted his head back, searching for control. This was wrong, it shouldn't be like this. This was supposed to be about *her*, not him. He wanted her to feel what he felt, wanted their first time together—*her* first time—to be special. Magical.

His hands closed over her shoulders in a gentle grip, the ends of her silky fine hair caressing his wrists. She looked up at him, brown eyes innocent and wide and filled with emotions she probably didn't want him to see.

The same emotions he felt tearing him apart inside. No, not tearing. Not unless tearing was supposed to make you feel all those girlie things, like being warm and mushy and gooey.

"Am I doing something wrong?"

Harland groaned at the uncertainty in her voice. He cleared his throat and shook his head, his mouth too dry to form words. He tightened the grip on her shoulders and shook his head again, turning so she was sprawled under his own body. And God, he was stretched out right between her legs, the tip of his cock so close. All he had to do was tilt his hips, just a little, and he'd be inside her—

No. Not yet.

"Nothing's wrong. I want you to feel what I feel."

She looked up at him, her wide eyes full of trust, and smiled. Damn her smile. It got him every single time, always had, for as long as he'd known her. Even when they were little kids and he'd chase her around the block, her smile would do him in, make him stumble and crash to a halt. And he'd be in so much trouble if any of his friends ever found that out.

But he wasn't with his friends. He was with *her*. His best friend. His soulmate.

And soon to be his lover.

"Nothing's wrong." He repeated the words in a hoarse choke and leaned down to kiss her. She wrapped her arms around his neck and leaned up, pressing the firmness of her small breasts against him. Then she tilted her hips and rubbed against him, nearly shattering what little control he had.

"Please, Harland. I'm ready."

"I don't want to hurt you."

"You won't."

"I will, we both know—"

She covered his mouth with two fingers and shook her head, the trust so clear in her deep eyes. "Only for a little bit. And not on purpose."

"No, not on purpose."

"Never on purpose. I know that."

Harland nodded and tried to swallow but his throat felt too tight, like it was clogged with something. He shifted his hips, the tip of his cock entering the tight warmth of her body. She stiffened under him then relaxed, her legs parting a little more.

He pushed again, hesitating when he reached the tight barrier protecting her innermost secret. Short nails dug into his arms but she didn't push him away. Instead, she wrapped her legs around his waist and tilted her hips toward his until the barrier broke and he was seated fully inside her.

"Harland." His name was part sigh, part cry, unleashing some primitive emotion deep inside him. He kissed her, long and hard, then braced himself on his elbows above her.

"I'll never hurt you again. Ever. I love you."

CHAPTER ONE

"Fuck!"

"Get your head in the fucking game, Day-glo, and that won't happen again." Jason Emory skated behind Harland, reaching for the puck that had just bounced off his ankle. Harland shot him a death glare then shook his foot. Yeah, his ankle still stung and yeah, he'd have a bruise there later. But Jason was right: if he'd been paying attention, the puck would have never hit him.

And he needed to be paying attention, now more than ever.

Training camp was over and he was still here. That had to count as some kind of miracle, especially after the last year. Screwing up on the ice, screwing up off the ice. Getting sent back here to the Bombers instead of playing pro with the Banners.

And his fucking head still wasn't in the game, not to where it needed to be. But damn it all, did it even matter? His chances of making it back to the pros were slim. He could see the writing on the wall, in each steady look the coaching staff sent his way. Like they were waiting for him to fuck up again. Because that's what he did: fucked things up.

Not just a little. Hell no, that would be too simple. He had to go out of his way to be a royal fuck up. Class A, head-of-the-line, *numero uno* fuck up. Go out of his way? Yeah, even that was a joke. He didn't have to go out of his way—it came natural. Almost like he was deliberately doing his best to destroy everything.

And why not? Wasn't that what he did best?

Harland tightened his grip on the stick and pushed off, gaining speed as he headed down the ice. Fast. Faster. Turning and skating backward, tapping with his stick. Jason shot the puck toward him and Harland tipped it with the blade, barely stopping it. He pulled it in closer, spun around, took a crazy shot at the net.

The puck hit the pipes and bounced off with a loud clang that echoed around the nearly-empty rink. Harland slid to a stop and swung the stick through the air like a bat, catching it against the pipes so hard it broke in two.

"Nice. Real nice." Jason slid to a stop just in front of him, covering Harland's legs with a spray of snow. He pushed his helmet back on his head and sent a stream of spit off to the side then glanced down at the broken stick. "How the fuck did you even miss that?"

Wasn't that the million-dollar question? Hell, if Harland knew the answer he'd be able to fix it. The problem was, he didn't know the answer. That's why he was here now, putting in more time on the ice. Not that it was doing any good. It wasn't. And he was very much afraid that if he didn't find the answer—soon—he might as well just give it up now.

Just pack it up and walk away. Yeah, that was one thing he *was* good at: walking away.

Not just walking away. Fucking things up beyond repair and *then* walking away. Yeah, he had to make sure there was no going back, not when he was done with something.

Harland reached for the broken half of the stick, not quite able to look Jason in the eye when he straightened.

"My game is totally fucked."

"You think?" Jason shot another stream of spit across the ice then fixed Harland with his patented intense stare from those creepy glacier-blue eyes. "When's the last time you got laid?"

"Really? This has nothing to do with getting a piece."

Jason shrugged. "You never know. Zach Mummert swears scoring off-ice helps him score on-ice."

"Yeah, right. Until his dick falls off from putting it in the wrong bunny. No thanks, I'll pass." Harland pushed away from the net, his stride slow and smooth.

"Since when do you have anything against bunnies?"

"I don't. But man, come on. The way Zach goes through them? And some of the ones he hooks up with? No way. He's just asking for trouble."

"Yeah, well. He must be doing something right because his shooting was on fire last season. You saw it."

Harland grunted but didn't say anything. What was there to say? Yeah, he saw it—from the bench where he'd spent most of his time. And fuck, he so didn't want to think about that. Not now. Thinking about it just pissed him off. Made him want to give up instead of fight.

He still had a chance. *That* was what he needed to focus on. Today. Tomorrow. Not yesterday. And he sure as hell didn't need to be thinking about six years ago, either. Or even three. No more thinking about the past. No more wishful thinking and playing what-if, either. That was just as bad, and part of what got him into this whole fucking mess.

"So." Jason slid around him, blocking him when he tried to reach for the latch on the door. "You ever going to tell me what happened?"

"With what?"

"You know what. What happened. Last year."

"Nothing happened."

"Bull fucking shit. We all watched you implode. It was worse than a fucking car wreck on I-83 at rush hour. So fess up, Day-glo. What happened?"

"Stop with the name. I hate that fucking name." Harland tried to push past him but Jason wouldn't budge.

"Too damn bad. So what happened?"

"Nothing. I'm not getting into it." Harland's eyes narrowed and his hand clenched into a tight fist inside his glove. One more time. That was all Jason had to do: ask him one more time, and everything would explode. Harland could feel it building inside him, hot and hard and growing, like he was suddenly a pressure cooker on the verge of malfunctioning.

Jason must have seen something in his eyes, or maybe in just the way Harland's body tensed. Something. He shook his head and stepped back, not saying anything as they moved off the ice.

Harland shouldn't have been surprised, though. It wasn't the first time someone had questioned him, although the others had at least been a little subtler. And it wouldn't be the last time, he was sure.

It wasn't a question he had any intention of answering. Ever. How could he, when he wasn't entirely sure of the answer? Yeah, he knew exactly what had happened, he wasn't that out of it. He kept fucking up until his life spiraled downhill. Until his whole game turned to shit. And the Banners had tired of it, had tired of giving him a chance to fix it, so they reassigned him back here. He had hoped, for one fleeting moment, that maybe he'd be picked up on waivers. That maybe another team would give him a chance.

Stupid. So fucking stupid. He'd cleared waivers—of course he did, because who else would want him?—and now here he was, back to playing in the minors. He just didn't know *why*. Why had his game—his life—gone to shit? What had happened to finally push him over the ledge to where he was now? Why had he stopped caring?

He knew the answer—he just didn't want to admit it. Didn't want to admit how weak and foolish he'd been.

How naïve and stupid. Yeah, he knew what happened—he just didn't want to think about it. And he was usually pretty good at ignoring it. Usually.

Except on those rare occasions when he stopped to let himself think, usually at night after he'd had a few drinks. That's when the ghosts appeared. Taunting, laughing. But he always managed to push them away, afraid to face them. To listen to them. Hell, afraid to really acknowledge them. Because what he'd done was childish and embarrassing. Because it showed how weak he was. No, better off to do what he did best and just ignore it. Forget it. Keep it in the past.

Except, for some reason, all he kept thinking about was the past.

Just like a few minutes ago, when he'd been so caught up thinking about that afternoon six years ago. He was damn lucky the puck hadn't been airborne; if it had been, he'd be dealing with a lot more than a potentially bruised ankle.

It all came down to one thing: he needed to get—and keep—his fucking head in the game.

"What time did you want to meet up later?" Jason's question pulled his mind back to the present. He tossed the pads to the bench then yanked the damp shirt over his head, using the time to figure out what the hell Jason was talking about.

Oh yeah. It was a Friday. A few of them were going out tonight, kicking things up a bit. Not that the night of the week made any difference, not to him. "I don't care. What time's good for you?"

"Want to meet early and grab something to eat first? I want to try that new place that opened by the Galleria."

"Yeah, we can do that." Harland grabbed the shower kit from his duffel and headed back to the shower. "You want me to pick you up or just meet there?"

"Meet there. I want my own car in case I hook up. And maybe we can find someone to hook you up with, too."

Harland forced a smile but didn't say anything. What was there to say? He couldn't tell his teammate he wasn't interested—hadn't been interested for the last nine months. No, probably even longer than that, if he was honest with himself.

Maybe Jason was right. Maybe that was what he needed. Meet someone, hook up, get laid. Get everything out of his system...whatever *everything* was.

Maybe.

And why the hell not? It wasn't like he was attached to anyone, hadn't been for over three years. Maybe hooking up was exactly what he needed.

CHAPTER TWO

The third drink was still in his hand, virtually untouched. He glanced down at it, briefly wondered if he should just put it down and walk away. It was still early, not even eleven yet. Maybe if he stuck it out for another hour; maybe if he finished this drink and let the whiskey loosen him up. Or maybe if he just paid attention to the girl draped along his side—

Maybe.

He swirled the glass in his hand and brought it to his mouth, taking a long sip of mostly melted ice. The girl next to him—what the fuck was her name?—pushed her body even closer, the swell of her barely-covered breast warm against the bare flesh of his arm.

"So you're a hockey player, right? One of Zach's teammates?"

Her breath held a hint of red wine, too sweet. Harland tried not to grimace, pushed the memories at bay as his stomach lurched. He tightened his grip on the glass—if he was too busy holding something, he couldn't put his arm around her or push her away—and glanced down. The girl looked like she was barely old enough to be in this place. A sliver of fright shot through him. They did card here, right? He wasn't about to be busted picking up someone underage, was he?

She had a killer body, slim and lean with just enough muscle tone in her arms and legs to reassure him that she didn't starve herself and probably worked out. Long tanned legs that went on for miles and dainty feet shoved into shoes that had to have heels at least five inches tall. He grimaced and briefly wondered how the hell she was even standing in them.

Of course, she *was* leaning against him, her full breasts pushing against his arm and chest. Maybe that was because she couldn't stand in those ridiculous heels. Heels like that weren't meant for walking—they were fuck-me heels, meant for the bedroom.

He looked closer, at her platinum-streaked hair carefully crafted in a fuck-me style and held in place by what had to be a full can of hairspray—or whatever the fuck women used nowadays. Thick mascara coated her lashes, or maybe they weren't even her real lashes, now that he was actually looking. No, he doubted they were real. That was a shame because from what he could see, she had pretty eyes, kind of a smoky gray set off by the shimmery eyeshadow coloring her lids. Hell, maybe those eyes weren't even real, maybe they were just colored contacts.

Fuck. Wasn't anything real anymore? Wasn't anyone who they really claimed to be? And why the fuck was he even worried about it when all he had to do was nod and smile and take her by the hand and lead her out? Something told him he wouldn't even have to bother with taking her home—or in his case, to a motel. No, he was pretty sure all he had to do was show her the backseat of his Expedition and that would be it.

Her full lips turned down into a pout and Harland realized she was waiting for him to answer. Yeah, she had asked him a question. What the hell had she asked?

Oh, yeah—

"Uh, yeah. Yeah, I play hockey." He took another sip of the watery drink and glanced around the crowded club. Several of his teammates were scattered around the bar, their faces alternately lit and shadowed by the colored lights pulsing in time to the music.

Jason pulled his tongue from some girl's throat long enough to motion to the mousy barmaid for a fresh drink. His gaze caught Harland's and a wide grin split his face when he nodded.

Harland got the message loud and clear. How could he miss it, when the nod was toward the girl hanging all over him? Jason was congratulating him on hooking up, encouraging him to take the next step.

Harland took another sip and looked away. Tension ran through him, as solid and real as the hand running along his chest. He looked down again, watched as slender fingers worked their way into his shirt. Nails scraped across the bare flesh of his chest, teasing him.

Annoying him.

He put the drink on the bar and reached for her hand, his fingers closing around her wrist to stop her. The girl looked up, a frown on her face. But she didn't move her hand away. No, she kept trying to reach for him instead.

"What'd you say your name was?"

"Does it matter?" Her lips tilted up into a seductive smile, full of heated promise as her fingers wiggled against his chest.

Did it matter? It shouldn't, not when all Harland had to do was smile back and release her hand and let her continue. Or take her hand and lead her outside. So why the fuck was he hesitating? Why didn't he do just that? That was why he came here, wasn't it? To let go. Loosen up. Hook up, get things out of his system.

No. That may be why Jason and Zach and the others were here and why they brought him along—but that wasn't why he was here. So yeah, her name mattered.

Maybe not to him, not in that sense. He just wanted to know she was interested in *him* and not what he did. That he wasn't just a trophy for her, a conquest to be bragged about to her friends in the morning.

He gently tightened his hand around her wrist and pulled her arm away, out of reach of his chest. "Yeah. It matters."

Something flashed in her eyes—surprise? Impatience? Hell if he knew. He watched her struggle with a frown, almost like she didn't want him to see it. Then she pasted another bright smile on her face, this one a little too forced, and pulled her arm from his grasp.

"It's Shayla." She stepped even closer, running her hand along his chest and down, her finger tracing the waistband of his jeans.

He almost didn't stop her. Temptation seized him, fisting his gut, searing his blood. It would be easy, so easy.

Too easy.

Then a memory of warm brown eyes, wide with innocence, came to mind. Clear, sharp and almost painful. Harland closed his eyes, his breath hitching in his chest as the picture in his mind grew, encompassing soft brown hair and perfect lips, curled in a trembling smile.

"Fuck." His eyes shot open. He grabbed the girl's hand—Shayla's—just as she started to stroke him through the worn denim. Her own eyes narrowed and she made no attempt to hide her frown this time.

"What are you doing?" Her voice was sharp, biting.

"I could ask you the same thing."

Her hand twisted in his grip. Once, twice. "Zach told me you needed to loosen up. That you were looking for a little fun."

Zach had put her up to this? Harland should have known. He narrowed his eyes, not surprised when the girl suddenly stiffened. Could she see his distaste? Sense his condemnation? He leaned forward, his mouth close to her ear, his voice flat and cold.

"Maybe you want me to whip my cock out right here so you can get on your knees and suck me off? Have everyone watch? Will that do it for you?"

She ripped her hand from his grasp and pushed him away, anger coloring her face. "You're a fucking asshole."

Harland straightened and fixed her with a flat smile. "You're right. I am."

She said something else, the words too low for him to hear, then spun around and walked away. Her steps were short, angry, and he had to bite back a smile when she teetered to the side and almost fell.

Loathing filled him, leaving him cold and empty. Not loathing of the girl—no, the loathing was all directed at himself. What the fuck was his problem?

The girl was right: he was a fucking asshole. A loathsome bastard.

Harland yanked the wallet from his back pocket and pulled out several bills, enough to cover whatever he'd had to drink and then some. He tossed down the watered whiskey, barely feeling the slight burn as it worked its way down his throat. Then he turned and stormed toward the door, ignoring the sound of his name being called.

He should have gone home, back to the three-bedroom condo he was now forced to share with the sorry excuse that passed for his father. But he wasn't in the mood to deal with his father's bullshit, not in the mood to deal with anything. So he drove, with no destination in mind, needing distance.

Distance from the spectacle he had just made of himself.

Distance from what he had become.

Distance from who he was turning into.

But how in the hell was he supposed to distance himself...from himself?

Harland turned into a residential neighborhood, driving blindly, his mind on autopilot. He finally stopped, eased the SUV against the curb, and cut the engine.

Silence greeted him. Heavy, almost accusing. He rested his head against the steering wheel and squeezed his eyes shut. He didn't need to look around to know where he was, didn't need to view the quiet street filled with small houses that showed years of wear. Years of life and happiness and grief and torment.

"Fuck." The word came out in a strangled whisper and he straightened in the seat, running one hand down his face. Why did he keep coming here? Why did he keep tormenting himself?

She didn't want to see him, would probably shove him off the small porch if he ever dared to knock on the door. He knew that, as sure as he knew his own name.

As sure as he knew that she'd be sickened by what he had become. Three years had gone by. Three years where he'd never bothered to even contact her. Hell, maybe he was being generous. Maybe he was giving himself more importance than he deserved. Maybe she didn't even remember him.

He rubbed one hand across his eyes and took a ragged breath, then turned his head to the side. The house was dark, just like almost every other house on the block. But he didn't need light to see it, not when it was so clear in his mind.

A simple cottage style home, with plain white siding that was always one season away from needing a new coat of paint. Flowerbeds filled with exploding color that hid the age of the house. A small backyard filled with more flowers and a picnic table next to the old grill, where something was always being fixed during the warmer months.

An image of each room filled his mind, one after the other, like a choppy movie playing on an old screen. Middle class, blue collar—but full of laughter and warm memories. He knew the house, better than his own.

He should. He'd spent more time there growing up than he had at his own run-down house the next street over. He had come here to escape, stayed because it was an oasis in his own personal desert of despair.

Until he had ruined even that.

He closed his eyes against the memories, shutting them out with a small whimper of pain. Then he started the truck and pulled away, trying to put distance between him and the past.

A past that was suddenly more real than the present.

CHAPTER THREE

"See you tomorrow!"

Courtney Williams smiled and nodded at the bus driver, unable to wave because her hands were full. She stepped away from the curb as the bus pulled away then turned with a sigh and headed down the street. The weight of the bags pulled on her arms, causing another ache in already sore muscles. She paused, readjusted her grip on one of the bags, then continued. Despite wearing her most comfortable shoes, her feet ached, the soles tight and the toes cramping.

Well, what had she expected? That was what happened from standing on her feet all day. And today had been longer than usual because she stayed to cover for her friend, Beth. It wasn't a hardship, not when the extra money would come in handy. And Beth would do the same thing for her if needed.

That was just one of the things she enjoyed about the hair salon where she worked. Everyone was family, always willing to help each other out when needed. Maybe they were dysfunctional sometimes—what family wasn't?—but in a pinch, they all pulled together.

Courtney paused again, blowing a strand of hair from her eyes before continuing. It was a nice day for a walk, maybe still a little warm for September but nowhere near as hot and muggy as it had been just a few weeks ago. The sun was already starting its slow decline behind her and there was something in the air—an edge, maybe, or just a bit of a chill that signaled change was coming.

Nothing more than a change in the weather, she told herself. Her life had changed enough already and she was quite happy with the way it was now, thank you very much. She didn't need—or want—any more change. Well, unless she hit the lottery. That would be one change she'd gladly accept.

She turned the corner, a small smile on her face. The lottery. Yeah, right. Not much chance of that ever happening. She pushed the thought from her mind, not allowing herself to dwell on fantasy for even a second. She didn't allow herself to indulge in fantasies or dreams or what-ifs, not anymore. Not after what had happened.

Courtney mentally rolled her eyes and called herself a fool for being so melodramatic. If she had made the comment out loud, anyone within hearing distance would think she'd suffered from some dark life-altering drama. Life altering, yes. But not traumatic. At least, not darkly traumatic, not now.

No, she was quite content with the way her life was now, thank you very much. She had her health, a job she loved, coworkers who were her friends, and her family.

And her family was what mattered most.

She turned the final corner and paused again, shifting the bags and rolling her shoulders to ease the ache in her neck. Her house was up ahead; in just a few more minutes she'd be inside, unpacking groceries. Then she'd go upstairs and relax, read a story—

Courtney stumbled to a stop, the breath leaving her in a rush. Her vision swam and for a brief second she thought she might actually fall over. She blinked her eyes and shook her head, telling herself she was seeing things. The weather must be hotter than she realized, making her hallucinate.

She had to be seeing things.

But no, the vision didn't waver. She wasn't hallucinating. A chill descended over her, numbing her to the point that she was afraid the bags would fall from her hands. An overwhelming urge to escape seized her. To drop the bags and turn around and run as far as her legs would carry her, then keep on going until she collapsed in a heap of rubbery nerves.

The urge died, replaced with a more immediate fear. Had the man resting on her front porch been inside? No. Surely her mother wouldn't have let him inside, wouldn't have told him—

Courtney took a deep breath, her mouth sucking in air like a drowning victim snatched from the water at the last possible minute. Her chest ached with the effort. Her hands shook and one bag nearly slipped from her sweaty grip.

No! The word was a silent scream in her mind and she repeated it to herself, more forcefully. *No!* He didn't have the power to do this to her, not again. Not unless she gave him that power.

And that was one thing she absolutely refused to do.

Her gaze narrowed, her vision focused only on the man sitting on her porch. She took another deep breath, not as shaky as the last one, and moved forward. One step in front of the other. Slow. Steady. One step at a time.

Just like she had done more than three years ago.

He must have heard her because his body stiffened. His head turned, a thick hank of dark blonde hair falling into pale, honey-brown eyes. She didn't need to see his eyes to know their color, not when she had looked into them for more years than she could remember.

Not when she looked into them each day.

Harland rubbed his hands along the denim of his jeans

then stood, slowly moving down the three steps of the small porch. He stopped, took a step forward, stopped again. Ran a hand through his hair, shoving it out of his eyes.

Courtney hesitated, the urge to turn and run even stronger. No! This was *her* house, *her* life. She wouldn't let him scare her away. Her hands fisted around the straps of the recycled grocery bags, so tight her nails dug into her palms. So tight she was afraid she was cutting off the circulation to her fingers.

They stood there, each staring at the other, neither of them saying a word. The warm air grew heavier, oppressive and smothering. Sweat beaded along her hairline; a small bead trickled down the back of her neck. The sensation felt like a bug crawling across her skin and she shivered.

Just that small movement was enough to release her from the odd spell that froze her in place only seconds before. She stepped onto the walkway leading to the house then stopped again. Would he move out of her way? Or would she need to push past him? Maybe she should just start swinging with one of the bags and—

She took another deep breath, reaching for a calm she didn't even come close to feeling. "You shouldn't be here, Harland."

"I just—" He stopped, his broad chest rising as he took a deep breath. He shifted, not quite looking at her, then ran a hand through his hair again. "I thought maybe we could talk."

Talk? He thought they could *talk*? Courtney swallowed against the tightness in her throat and shook her head. "You said everything there was to say three years ago. Or don't you remember?"

Why did her voice have to break? Why was there so much emotion in those words? There shouldn't be any. Or, if there had to be emotion, it should be anger—not sorrow, not pain. Certainly not regret. She swallowed again and moved forward, ready to push past him. He took a step to the side, blocking her. One hand reached out, stretching toward the bags.

"Let me help with those—"

"No." She stepped back so quickly she almost tripped over the uneven concrete of the walkway. His hand closed over her elbow, steadying her. The heat of his touch shot through her, almost paralyzing her, causing her breath to catch and her pulse to soar. No. No, she would *not* react like this to him. She wouldn't allow it.

She pulled her arm from his grasp and stepped to the side, away from him. "Don't touch me."

"Courtney, I—"

"No. I don't want to hear it. You said everything there was to say the last time we saw each other." She kept walking, feeling the weight of his gaze between her shoulder blades as she hurried up the steps. The door opened from the inside and Courtney said a small prayer of thanks when her mother stepped forward to open the screen door. She took one of the bags then carefully studied Courtney's face before turning her dark gaze to the sidewalk outside.

"Courtney, maybe you should—"

"No, Mom. There's nothing to say to him."

"You know that's not true."

Courtney pushed her way deeper into the house, heading for the small kitchen. She dropped the bag to the floor then gripped the counter with both hands.

Breathe. Just breathe.

Muffled voices spoke from somewhere behind her. She couldn't hear the words, didn't need to. Her mother was saying something to Harland, her voice quiet and soothing. Then she heard the click of the door closing, followed by the subdued sound of her mother's steps on the tile floor.

Courtney took another deep breath then released her grip on the counter and reached for the bag on the floor. A hand closed over her shoulder, the touch firm but gentle.

"I'll get that. You get some water. You look pale."

Was it any wonder? If anything, Courtney was surprised she wasn't more than just pale. Her heart raced in her chest; the quick *thumpa-thumpa-thumpa* beating against her sternum physically hurt. Her skin felt hot, flushed in spite of the chilled sweat covering her. Her hands shook as she reached for the handle of the refrigerator and she stopped, curling them into tight fists as her mother moved around her, putting things away.

"How—" Her voice cracked and she swallowed, tried again. "How long was he here?"

Her mother sighed and she could hear the hesitation in her voice. "Almost two hours."

Two hours? But why? Why show up at all? Now, after all this time, after everything.

Courtney spun around, her eyes narrowing as she studied the back of her mother's head. "You didn't let him in? You didn't tell him?"

Cold fear gripped her when her mother's back stiffened. Then she turned around, her gaze soft and understanding. "No. He didn't come inside. And I didn't tell him anything." Her mother paused, her mouth pursing in quiet censure. "You need to be the one to tell him."

"No. No, absolutely not."

"Courtney, he has a right to know."

"He gave up that right when he said what he did. When he walked away. You know that."

"It's been over three years. Things change. And you know as well as I do why he said those things."

Courtney shook her head, as if the motion would be enough to make everything go away. To just disappear, like none of it had ever happened. No, she couldn't think that—*wouldn't* think that.

"It doesn't matter, Mom. Not anymore. Not after everything—" Her voice broke again and she sucked in a shaky breath, wishing that the emotions battering her would just go away. Why? Why had he shown up, now of all times?

And why was she reacting this way? Pain and hurt and anger and regret and sorrow. And, deep below all of that, a tiny sliver of hope. That was the emotion she needed to crush. Hope? Even now, after everything, her heart could feel hope? She was such a fool.

Something barreled into her legs, nearly knocking her over. Courtney grabbed the counter to catch herself then looked down at the soft grunt. A smile spread across her face and she lowered herself to the floor, sitting cross-legged as she leaned against the cabinet. Noah climbed in to her lap, his hands gently patting at the tears on her cheeks. Then his fingers slowly moved, his small brow creased in concentration as worry filled his light brown eyes.

His father's eyes.

Why cry?

Courtney brushed the dampness from her cheeks and forced a smile to her face, answering him. *Because I can.*

Noah's face scrunched up, his mouth opening in a silent giggle. Then he placed one hand on each side of her cheek and gifted her with a loud kiss. She pulled him into a hug, holding his small body close to hers.

"Every boy needs their father, Courtney." Her mother's voice was gentle despite the admonishment lacing it. She didn't bother whispering—there was no need to.

Courtney tightened her arms around Noah and looked up at her mother. "Because that worked so well for Harland?"

"Harland isn't like his father."

"Isn't he?" Courtney's voice was bitter, accusing. Guilt flooded her as soon as the words came out. No, Harland wasn't like his father. At least, she would have never thought so all those years ago. But now—

No. Even now he wasn't. Despite the last few years, despite what had been said and done, despite not seeing him in so long—she knew he wasn't. But he could be. Just two steps in the wrong direction and he could be.

And that's what scared her the most.

CHAPTER FOUR

Harland jammed the key into the lock, opened the door...and stopped. Anger swept through him and he tamped it down, his back teeth grinding so hard he was surprised they didn't disintegrate.

The volume from the television was turned high enough to rattle his abused back teeth. An empty pizza box, complete with congealed grease, was tossed on the floor. Empty beer cans rested on their sides inside the box, along with a pile of cigarette butts and ashes.

Harland slammed the door shut as hard as he could. The man sprawled on the sofa jumped; the arm carelessly tossed over his eyes dropped to the floor and he rolled to his side. But he didn't fall off. No, that would be hoping for too much.

Harland dropped his bag to the floor with a thud and stormed over to the sofa. "What did I tell you about smoking in here?"

"What?" The man's voice was scratchy, like he hadn't used it in a while. He pushed himself up then ran one large hand through his graying hair. Harland's eyes focused on the hand: square, blunt, the fingers long and thick, the nails lined with shadows of grease. Had they ever not been lined with grease? Not that he could remember.

"I told you I didn't want you smoking in here. The place reeks. And couldn't you even bother to clean up your shit?"

"Yeah. Whatever." His father leaned forward, reaching for the can of beer sitting on the coffee table. He drained it with one long swallow then crushed the can in his hand and tossed it with the others before turning the television volume down.

"I just said—"

"I heard you. I'm getting it." His father leaned over, scooping up the old pizza box and folding the lid closed. He stood and pushed past Harland on the way to the kitchen. Why the fuck was he still here? Why was he here, period? Because Harland didn't have the balls to kick him out when he showed up a few weeks after he'd been sent back here to York, that was why. His old man had just shown up, out of the blue. Somehow wormed his way into staying here—because he knew his son wouldn't say no.

Harland had to stand up to him. Had to do something, anything. This couldn't continue, couldn't keep going like it was, not if Harland expected to keep his sanity intact. He'd tell him. Now, tonight. Just tell his old man that enough was enough and he had to leave—

"Why the hell are you home so late?"

Harland blew out a breath, knowing he wouldn't say anything, couldn't say anything. He never could, not when it came to his old man. "I stayed after practice."

"Really?" His father pulled another beer from the refrigerator then leaned against the doorway, his gaze penetrating, flat. "So you decide to get your head in the game *after* you fuck everything up? Should have thought about that before."

Harland clenched his jaw again then retrieved his bag from the floor. How the hell did his father expect him to answer that? Yeah, he had fucked up. Everyone knew it.

27

But not everyone kept throwing it in his face like his old man.

"I'm jumping in the shower then going out."

"Where to now?"

"Just out. Why? Are you suddenly keeping track of what I do?"

"Somebody has to. You can't afford any more mistakes, son. Not as long as there's a chance you can make it back to the pros."

"Yeah, sure." Harland tossed the bag over his shoulder then pinned his father with a hard glare. Eyes nearly identical to his own stared back at him, void of all emotion. Is that what Harland looked like to others? Cold? Flat? Emotionless?

He didn't want to believe it. *Couldn't* believe it. He already resembled his father too much physically. Looking at him was like looking in a mirror that magically aged the viewer twenty-five years. They had the same eyes, same hair; the same facial features and the same build. His father's body was finally showing the signs of time and harsh living but, in some odd way, that only made the resemblance more striking, more pronounced.

No. It was bad enough Harland looked so much like him—he didn't want to *be* like him, too.

"What are you staring at?"

"Nothing." Harland shook his head and moved toward the hallway.

"Just remember what I said: no more mistakes."

"Yeah, Dad. I heard you. That's why I'm practicing my ass off."

"I'm not just talking about the game. I mean *all* mistakes."

"Like what?" As soon as the words left his mouth, he wished he could take them back. Getting into a conversation—about anything—with his father right now was the last thing he needed.

"Everything. You have condoms, right?"

"Fucking shit." Harland nearly lost his grip on the bag. Had he heard right? Yeah, he had. His father was still staring at him, his own jaw clenched, the warning clear in his gaze. Harland shook his head. "I am not having this conversation with you. Ever. Christ. I can't believe—no, forget it. I'm not doing it—"

"All I'm saying is you can't afford any more mistakes. Find a girl, fuck her if you want, but take precautions."

"What the fuck, Dad? I'm not discussing my sex life with you. What I do is none of your damn business—"

"It is when you make mistakes. I'm only looking out for you, son. Just like I did a few years ago with that one girl."

"What the hell are you talking about now?"

"That girl you used to run around with."

The blood in Harland's veins froze instantly. Icy tendrils of anxiety spread through his limbs and he took a step forward. "Are you talking about Courtney?"

His father took a long swallow of beer then raised the can in a salute of acknowledgement. "Yeah, that's the one. Never could remember the little sleaze's name. Never understood what you saw in her, either."

"What are you talking about? What did you do?" Each word was clipped, precise and cold. His father didn't notice, just moved past him back into the living room.

"You know what I did. That whole pregnancy thing. I set that straight, didn't I? To think she tried blaming that on you."

Emotion slammed into Harland, nearly doubling him over. He didn't want to think about that time all those years ago. Didn't want to remember all the angry words and accusations. Didn't want to remember the emptiness he felt at her admission. Hollow, cold. Betrayed. Like he'd lost his best friend.

More than his best friend. So much more.

He laughed, the sound short and bitter. Didn't want to remember? Christ, he couldn't *stop* remembering. Isn't that why he stopped by her place last week? Like maybe she was the missing puzzle piece to whatever the fuck was going on with him. Like seeing her would somehow make things right, or at least let him move on.

He'd been a fool—in more ways than one. Seeing her hadn't helped. If anything, it had only made things worse, made him feel even more lost and adrift than he had been before seeing her.

"Don't bring Courtney up. Ever. I'm not talking about her."

"Didn't expect you to, Har." His father grinned and sat back on the leather sofa, getting comfortable. Probably settling in for the night, just like he had every night since moving in.

"Still can't believe she tried to pass that bastard off as yours. Well, I guess she learned her lesson, didn't she?"

"She didn't pass anything off, Dad. She didn't have it." Had his father noticed the strained tone of his words? How he had to force them through numb lips? No, of course not. His father was too busy flipping through the channels to pay attention.

"Is that what she told you? Figures." His father glanced over his shoulder then shrugged. "No, she had it alright. No idea whose it is, though. All I can say is good riddance. You don't need to be taking care of someone else's bastard, not when you need to focus on your career."

Harland heard the words but didn't understand them. Not at first. His brain caught each word, examined it, moved to the next one. Slowly, like his mind had been encased in molasses, unable to process things. Then, one word at a time, he repeated the words to himself. Over and over until comprehension sunk in.

He dropped the bag and stormed over to the sofa, his fists resting on the edge of it as he leaned over his father. "What did you say?"

"What is your problem? Stop leaning over me like that. You're in the way." His father tried pushing him away but Harland didn't move.

"Are you saying Courtney had the baby?"

"Yeah. What about it?"

"She told me she was—" Harland swallowed the words, unable to say them. Unable to forget the anguished screams and accusations from that long-ago day. "She said she wasn't going to have it."

"Well she did. What do you care? She told you it wasn't yours. It's not your problem."

Problem? Was that what his father thought? Harland straightened, fought to stay upright when his legs wanted to buckle beneath him. His stomach tightened and lurched, threatening to rebel against him.

Yes, Courtney had said it wasn't his...after he had accused her, over and over and over. Because he had let his father convince him she was seeing someone else. Because he had believed his own flesh-and-blood was looking out for him.

So he had confronted her, accused her. Wouldn't leave it alone until she admitted everything he was saying was true. But deep down, a part of him had never really believed her, even after his father had convinced him. Even after Courtney had admitted it. A part of him had always hoped...it didn't matter what he hoped. It was done. Over. The words and accusations had cut too deep, left wounds that would never heal.

And now his father was telling him that she'd had the baby? Like it was no big deal. Like it was nothing more than an inconvenient problem—somebody else's problem.

Harland took another step back, sucking in deep breaths, trying to control the sudden shaking that seized him. He turned, stumbled, righted himself.

"Where the hell are you off to now?"

His father's voice was nothing more than an irritating buzz in his ears and he waved it off. He needed to get out of here, get away. He needed air. He needed to clear his head and think. To be by himself. But more than any of that, he needed to find out the truth.

CHAPTER FIVE

Breathe. He needed to breathe.

Fuck that. He needed answers.

Harland banged his fist against the door again. Hard. Over and over. He knew someone was home: the lights were on, he could hear the muted sounds of the television coming from the back of the house.

Why weren't they answering the door?

An image came to mind, devastating in its clarity: Courtney, curled on the edge of the sofa, wrapped in the arms of another man. Too preoccupied to hear the banging on the door.

"Fuck." Harland ran a hand through his hair and forced himself to calm down. Courtney wasn't like that. Yeah, it had been several years, she could be seeing someone. Probably *was* seeing someone. But this was her mother's house, she wouldn't—

Except she *had*, with him. Numerous times.

He curled his hand into a fist and banged the door again, harder this time. Something else drove him, something besides his father's revelation. An almost desperate need to see for himself, to prove Courtney was alone. If she would just open—

The door swung open, revealing a surprised—and irritated—face. Soft and oval, just now starting to show the signs of a full life. Soft brown hair, gently threaded with an occasional strand of silver, curled around the aging face. The eyes widened briefly in surprise then narrowed.

"Harland. Good Lord, I thought the door was ready to come off the hinges. What on earth are you trying to do?"

"Mrs. Williams, I'm sorry." Harland tried to step forward but she didn't move, didn't step back to let him in. "Is—is Courtney here?"

Pale lips pursed in a small frown and for a brief second, Harland actually expected her to close the door in his face. "So it's 'Mrs. Williams' now, is it? I remember a time when you used to call me something else."

Mom. The memory slammed into him, just one more thing to add to the long list of things making it hard for him to breathe. Harland pushed the memories—and the accompanying emotions—away, sucked in a raged breath.

"I—" He hesitated, started again. "Is Courtney here? Please. I need to see her."

Christina Williams' hands, small and gentle, tightened around the edge of the door. She threw a glance over her shoulder then looked back at Harland. Something like sorrow passed across her face and she slowly shook her head. "But I don't think she wants to see you, Harland. You should just go home."

The door started to swing closed. Harland reached out and placed the flat of his hand against the thick wood, stopping it from closing in his face. "Please."

Maybe it was the quiet desperation in his voice, or the panic he knew was etched on his face. For whatever reason, she finally relented and opened the door wider, stepping back to let him in. "I'll go see—"

He pushed past her, his gaze raking the empty entranceway, the empty living room just beyond it. He turned, ready to head toward the stairs.

"Harland Anthony Day. Don't you *dare* go tearing through my house." A hand clamped around his arm, the strength surprising him. He felt himself being tugged away from the stairs, toward the small eat-in kitchen area. She led him to a chair and forced him to sit. "You know better."

"But—"

"No buts. You know better." She stepped back, her hands braced on slim hips, and stared at him. Almost like she wasn't sure what to do with him, wasn't sure how he had suddenly ended up sitting at the kitchen table.

The same table where he had spent so many nights while he was growing up. Eating dinner. Doing homework. Playing games. Like any normal happy family. Only they hadn't been his family, not really. Not by blood.

She finally sighed, a drawn-out sound full of weariness. "You stay here and I'll see if Courtney wants to see you. And don't you dare move from this chair. Do you understand me?"

"Yes ma'am."

"Hm." She looked like she wanted to say something else but she didn't, just turned and left, leaving him there, alone with nothing but memories—and regrets.

He propped his elbows on the scarred wooden surface and dropped his head into his hands. His fingers dug into his scalp, squeezing, trying to keep the memories at bay.

Too many memories. Christ, he'd spent more time here than he had at his own place growing up. He'd found a home here, warm and welcoming, full of laughter and happiness. So different from the cold and empty house where he lived, his father hardly ever home, his mother gone, her whereabouts unknown.

Voices drifted down the stairs, the words garbled but the tone unmistakable. Anger, surprise. He heard one word, clear and determined.

No.

That had been Courtney's voice, thick with emotion

but not lacking in strength. His gut twisted and lurched again. Would she see him? And if she did, would she tell him the truth? Not the truth he had fooled himself into believing all those years ago—he wanted the real truth.

Another thought assailed him, nearly doubling him over. He wasn't sure why he hadn't considered it before. Maybe because he hadn't been thinking clearly—he still wasn't, not really. Maybe because his mind was still trying to deny what his heart knew—what his heart had always known, if he'd only listened.

His father had said she'd *had* the baby. But had she kept it—or given it up for adoption? He would have heard if she'd kept it...wouldn't he? Would she have said something the other day? Wouldn't her mother have said something?

No. Why would they, after everything had happened? Why would they think it was any of his business?

Christ. Was the baby upstairs now? No, not a baby. Not anymore.

A chill settled over him. His hands began shaking, then his whole body. Small tremors at first, there and gone, replaced by an uncontrollable shivering. It was like he'd been dipped in water then forced onto the ice in nothing but a pair of skates. He couldn't get warm, couldn't stop shaking, couldn't get his mind to focus on any one thing.

No, that wasn't entirely true. Images he didn't want to acknowledge flashed through his mind with the intensity of a strobe light. Harsh. Bright. Painful. He closed his eyes, trying to shut everything out, and only succeeded in making the images clearer.

Footsteps echoed on the stairs behind him and rang in his head, an auditory backdrop to the flashing images. Harland stood, the chair scraping across aged linoleum. The room around him spun and he leaned forward, gripping the edge of the table so he wouldn't fall. He pulled icy air into his lungs, held it until he was certain he wouldn't fall over.

Then he turned around, slowly, afraid of what he'd see. Afraid of what he wouldn't see.

Courtney moved from the stairs, her own steps slow and measured. Her normally healthy complexion was pale, her face drawn, her lips pressed tightly together. Brown eyes, several shades darker than his own, fixed on his. The fear and anxiety he felt were reflected in those eyes and he looked away, afraid of what else he might see.

Then his gaze landed on the child in her arms. A boy, not quite three years old. The child wrapped his small arms around his mother's neck then turned his head—and Harland realized he was looking into a mirror, seeing himself at that age.

His legs buckled, finally giving out. He reached for the table, the chair—anything. But his hands were numb, his vision swimming. And then he was on his knees, doubled over in pain, his lungs fighting for air as his mind fought to accept what his heart already knew.

What his heart had known as soon as his father had told him. No, before that, even. What his heart had known all those years ago, what he had blocked out and refused to believe.

He was a father.

CHAPTER SIX

Courtney didn't move except to tighten her arms around Noah. All she could do was watch as Harland dropped to his knees, as he wrapped his arms around his waist and gulped for air.

Part of her wanted to be immune to his distress. To turn her back on him and walk away and pretend she felt nothing. But another part of her—a very small piece of her—wanted to rush forward and take him in her arms. To rock him and tell him everything would be alright, much like she still rocked Noah at times.

She cursed herself for her weakness and refused to move. Tell him everything would be alright? Why? Why would she even consider doing that? Nothing was *alright* and hadn't been for several years. Nothing would ever be the same again, ever. So why should she comfort him after everything that had happened? After everything he had done?

She heard a gasp behind her, sensed her mother coming to a stop on the bottom step.

"Harland!" Her mother's voice was laced with concern and surprise as she moved past Courtney.

"Mom, don't." There must have been something in Courtney's voice, some sense of the emotions warring inside her, because her mother actually listened to her. A small victory, when she knew how much she still cared for Harland.

The victory was short-lived. Her mother gave her a pointed look then moved forward. She reached Harland, bent down and placed a slender arm around his shoulders. Courtney couldn't hear what she was saying, not when the words were quietly spoken in Harland's ear.

Noah stiffened in her arms then started to push against her, his legs kicking. He made a small grunt, the noise nothing more than a breathless wheeze as his hand made a single sign.

Down.

"Noah, no." Courtney shook her head but he continued kicking, his back arching. What in the world? She finally gave up and bent over, lowering him to his feet. He pushed away and hurried toward his grandmother.

No, not toward his grandmother. Toward Harland.

Courtney made a small cry of dismay but that only succeeded in capturing Harland's attention. He sat back on his heels, his eyes wide with shock as Noah came to a sudden stop in front of him.

Courtney stepped forward, ready to grab her son and whisk him away to safety. Her mother waved her off with a stern look and a shake of her head. Courtney fisted her hands, wishing she had never listened to her mother. If it had been up to her, she'd still be upstairs with Noah, locked safely in her room until Harland left.

But her mother had been so adamant, so unwavering, that Courtney had no choice but to give in.

He deserves to know.

Did he? After everything he had said, everything he had accused her of? And what would he do with that knowledge? That's what worried Courtney the most. Not just worried: that's what terrified her.

She watched, unable to move, unable to breathe. Noah took another hesitant step toward Harland then stopped, his head tilting to the side as he studied the man in front of him. Not for the first time, Courtney wished he wasn't quite such a curious child.

Harland's stunned gaze moved from Noah to her. "He's mine."

He made the two words a statement but she didn't miss the question underneath. Courtney crossed her arms in front of her, her fingers biting into the flesh of her arms, and said nothing. Harland watched her for a long minute then slowly nodded. Had he answered his own question? Or was the nod for another reason, one she didn't understand?

He looked back at Noah, already dismissing her. Then he shifted so he was sitting cross-legged on the floor. A hesitant smile played at the corners of his lips. "Hey there, Little Man. How are you?"

Was that really Harland's voice? Soft, gentle. Hesitant. It was like a different man was speaking, one she didn't know. Except that wasn't true. She'd heard him talk like that before, when things had been different. When life had been different.

So much time had passed and so many different things had happened that she had forgotten that side of him. And she didn't want to remember.

"What's your name?" Harland's voice again, still soft and hesitant. Noah placed his hand against Harland's mouth then turned back to look at her, curiosity clear in the honey-brown eyes that were so much like his father's.

Courtney moved closer and had to restrain herself from scooping Noah into her arms. "His name is Noah. Noah Robert."

Harland glanced up at her then looked away, his gaze softening. "Hi Noah Robert Day. I'm—"

"It's Williams. Noah Robert *Williams*. Not *Day*."

Anger flashed in Harland's eyes, followed by what she

thought might be sorrow. No, she must be reading into things. Why would he feel sorrow after being so adamant that the child she carried wasn't his? She expected him to say something, to argue with her or make some biting comment that would leave her reeling. Instead he looked away and ran the tip of his finger along Noah's nose.

"Hi Noah. I'm Harland. Can you say Harland?"

Noah looked at her once more, curiosity now mingled with delight. She made several slow signs for Noah, watched as he struggled to mimic them. Harland's eyes narrowed at the exchange, the silent question clear in his gaze.

Courtney took a deep breath and moved even closer, finally giving into the urge to pull her son into her arms. She dropped a kiss on the top of his head. The baby-fine hair was smooth against her lips, fresh and clean from his recent bath. She kissed him again then shifted so his weight was resting on her hip. She focused her steady gaze on Harland when she spoke.

"Noah is deaf, Harland. He can't hear."

So many different emotions flashed through his eyes: anger, bewilderment, shock. Pity. Pain. And yes, blame. At her? Himself? She didn't know, couldn't tell because all the emotions disappeared in one slow blink. If Courtney hadn't been looking—hadn't specifically been watching him just so she could see any reaction—it would be hard to say she had seen any emotions at all. But she *had* been watching, just for that reason. Because she knew how easy it was for Harland to hide what he was feeling. That, at least, hadn't changed.

It never mattered how well he'd his them, though. She'd still been able to read his emotions, all those years ago. He could hide what he felt from everyone else but not from her. Never from her. Could she still do it? Still sense—still *feel*—what was underneath that aloof surface?

She was afraid to try, afraid to look too closely. Afraid of the answer.

"Okay young man. Bed time." Her mother's voice pulled her back to the present. She started, surprised to realize she had been standing there, her gaze locked on Harland.

Noah made a soft wheezing sound then pressed a sloppy kiss against her cheek. Courtney smiled as he practically jumped from her arms into his grandmother's then bounced up and down with silent glee. He finally settled in her arms then looked back at Harland and waved.

And then they were alone.

Silence settled over them, tense and still. Courtney's arms felt empty, awkward, and she wasn't sure what to do with them. She didn't know what to say, or if she should even move. Run upstairs and hide? That's what she wanted to do. But she couldn't, not with Harland still sitting on the floor a few feet away.

He finally moved, standing with a muffled grunt. She almost teased him about getting old, like she used to do when they were youner, then savagely bit the words back. Those days were gone, long dead and buried.

He watched her for a long minute then reached for one of the chairs. "Sit. We need to talk."

"I don't think—"

"We need to talk." There was no mistaking the command in his voice. Courtney hesitated. She didn't want to talk to him. Not now, not ever. Hadn't they said everything they had to say that night over three years ago?

There was no mistaking the silent demand in his expression, though. And looking at him, she realized this wasn't the same boy—man—she had known a lifetime ago. He was bigger, broader through the chest and shoulders. His hair was just a little darker than she remembered. And longer than he used to wear it, especially in the front where it fell over his broad forehead. His face was leaner, more sculpted, carrying a scar or two that hadn't been there before. Even his hands and wrists were larger, the muscles more defined than she remembered. From playing hockey, of course.

She hadn't wanted to but she'd kept up with his career once he moved to the pros. Not fanatically, not seeking out and hanging on every game or every single piece of gossip about him. But she had followed enough to watch his play grow and mature—and to watch it implode for no apparent reason.

The man standing in front of her, watching her with such a direct and commanding gaze, wasn't the smiling yet serious boy she had fallen in love with. He was someone completely different. Harder, more remote. A total stranger.

She needed to remember that, even as she finally gave in and took the chair he held out for her. Was it her imagination, or did some of the tension seem to leave him? He had probably expected a fight. As much as she would have loved to give him one, it wasn't in her best interest. No, the sooner they talked, the sooner he would leave.

And the sooner he'd be gone from her life once more.

"Noah is my son." The words were brisk, forceful, with no hint of question in them. Courtney folded her arms in front of her and stared at him.

"Is he?"

"You know he is."

"Not according to you, I don't. I seem to recall you being pretty adamant that he wasn't yours when I told you I was pregnant." By some miracle, the words had come out clear and strong, with no hint of the emotions that were battering her inside. She dug her fingers deeper into the flesh of her arms, needing to hide their shaking from Harland's careful gaze.

Maybe she wasn't as successful at hiding the emotion as she thought because sorrow and regret flashed in Harland's eyes. He didn't blink them away or try to hide them when he spoke.

"I was wrong. I—" He took a deep breath and looked

away. "I should have never said what I did."

"But you did."

The words hung between them, heavy and final. Did he really expect her to pretend his accusations hadn't mattered? That it was in the past, forgotten and forgiven? Maybe there were other people out there who could forgive and forget, who could move on and pretend the bad things never happened. Bigger people, forgiving people.

She wasn't one of them.

"I—" His gaze slid to hers, moved away once more. "He's my son. I want to be part of his life."

Fear swept through her, cold and paralyzing. But she couldn't—wouldn't—let him see it. She swallowed, focused on keeping her voice steady. "You should have thought about that three years ago."

"You can't keep me out of his life, Courtney. I'm his father. I have a right to be part of his life."

"You were never in his life. Ever. You weren't there when he was born. You didn't sit up nights with him when he was sick, when he wouldn't eat or drink or sleep. You weren't here when he got his first tooth or took his first step." Her voice shook with anger and she leaned forward, no longer worried about hiding her emotions.

"You weren't there when the doctors told me he would never hear. You didn't—*don't*—struggle with learning how to teach him how to communicate. You aren't here, dealing with his appointments and lessons and everything else that goes on. So don't you *dare* tell me you have a right to be in his life. Not after everything you said and did. You haven't earned that right. You *don't have* that right and you never will!"

"Bullshit!" Harland slammed his hand against the table, both the sound and his outburst making her jump. "I have every right. I'm his father!"

"Not according to his birth certificate, you're not."

"What?" Harland sat back as if she had slapped him.

The color drained from his face and his voice shook when he spoke. "Who's listed as his father?"

Courtney wanted to lie, to toss out some random name just to hurt him. To make him feel just a small fraction of the pain she had felt. But she couldn't. She sat back in the chair, suddenly drained, and focused her gaze on the surface of the table. "His father is listed as 'unknown'."

Harland's hand flattened against the table, his fingers bending as the tips dug into the hard surface. She heard him exhale, saw his hand finally, slowly, relax. And she saw the way his fingers trembled before he moved his hand away, out of her line of sight.

"You hate me so much that you would do that?"

It hadn't been her choice: it had been the state of Pennsylvania's since she was an unmarried woman and there was no Acknowledgement of Paternity. But she wasn't going to tell him that. Better to let him think she hated him that much, if only to keep him out of their lives, like he had been. Better for him, better for her. Better for Noah.

"Courtney." Just her name, harsh and raw. She shook her head, refusing to look at him, and heard the ragged exhalation of a deep breath. "Courtney. He's my son. I want to be part of his life."

And oh God, she couldn't do this anymore. Not with Harland sitting so close, not with the myriad of emotions coming off him in waves and assaulting her. It was too much, brought back too many memories, awakened too many dreams.

She wrapped her arms around her middle and shook her head again. "You need to leave, Harland."

"Courtney, I—"

"Please. I can't...I can't do this. Not now. Please."

Maybe it was the way her voice broke. Or maybe they still had enough of a connection that he could sense her own tumultuous emotions, the same way she could sense his. She didn't know what the reasons were and she didn't care. It didn't matter what the reasons were because Harland slowly pushed away from the table and stepped around her.

Her body tensed, her shoulders drawing tight around her ears when he stopped behind her. Gently, the touch sensed more than felt, he pressed a featherlight kiss against the top of her head. She gasped, the air sticking in her throat and nearly choking her, but he didn't say anything. Less than a minute later, she heard the sound of the door closing behind him as he left.

Courtney dropped her head to the table and released the barriers she had struggled so hard to keep in place. The tears came, raw and burning but far from cleansing. So far.

Because she knew, as certain as she knew who her son's father was, that Harland would be back. And she was very much afraid that she wouldn't be able to keep pushing him away.

CHAPTER SEVEN

Dig in.

Push off.

Harder. Faster. Back and forth, over and over again.

Harland drifted to a stop and bent over at the waist, his stick resting against his knees. Sweat ran down his face and coated his body. A drop fell from his chin and landed on the ice at his feet, spreading out. He stared at it, watching as it slowly froze and disappeared.

Part of him wished he could disappear as quickly.

He straightened and took a deep breath then wiped his face against the damp material of the practice jersey. He should take a break, get hydrated.

No, fuck that. He didn't want to stop. If he stopped, he'd start to think. Thinking was the last thing he wanted to do.

He skated to the other side of the ice and grabbed the bucket of pucks sitting near the player's bench. One after the other, he lined them up on the blue line, six inches apart. Then, without thinking, he just started shooting. One, two, three.

Again, over and over, mindless shooting toward the

net. The sound of rubber hitting metal rang through the empty rink, taunting him. Such an odd sound: hollow, vacant, empty.

A sound his son would never hear.

"Fuck!" Harland whirled in a tight circle, sucking in heavy breaths. His heart pounded in his chest, too heavy beneath the weight of his pads. From the exertion, or something else?

The sense of unreality hadn't left him all week. One day, everything had been as close to his new normal as it could be. Then, several hours later, his entire life had been turned upside down and inside out. He was skidding out of control, with no idea of what *normal* was anymore—and with no idea what he wanted to do about it.

Courtney wouldn't answer his calls. Mrs. Williams wouldn't even answer the door. He'd finally stopped going over after practices because he was afraid of having the police called on him, something he worried was a real possibility. What the hell would he have done then?

What the hell was he supposed to do now?

He didn't know. Fuck, he didn't even know what it was he *wanted* to do. Noah was his son. Harland had a right to be a part of his life.

Didn't he?

"You ready for that ambulance?"

The question echoed through the empty rink and Harland whirled in surprise, nearly losing his balance. Aaron Malone stood a few feet away, carelessly leaning against the boards. He was dressed in black workout pants and a frayed gray sweatshirt. Skates adorned his feet and a stick was held loosely in one bare hand.

Harland straightened, tried to act nonchalant. "I didn't hear you come in."

"No shit." Aaron pushed away from the boards in a slow glide, stopping a foot away. He raised his arm and Harland noticed the sports drink in his hand. "You might want this before you keel over."

"Yeah. Thanks." Harland accepted the bottle, uncapped it and drained half of it in one long swallow. His gaze met the other man's then darted away.

He didn't know Aaron that well. Hell, there were several players he didn't really know that well. Harland was still the odd man out, despite being part of the team. They played together—if you could call what he did at the end of last season *playing*—and they practiced together. And yeah, a few of them hung out together, went out to drink and carry on. But he wasn't really close to many of the guys, except maybe Jason and Zach.

And Aaron wasn't one to usually go out and party and carry on. He was the oldest guy on the team, somewhere in his early thirties. Harland had no idea how many years he'd been playing, how many teams—pro and minors—he'd played for. Would the Bombers be the last? Christ, wasn't that a depressing fucking thought.

"Killing yourself isn't going to help."

"What?"

Aaron nodded at the pucks scattered around the net then back at Harland. "You heard me. Whatever you're trying to do, trying to prove, trying to forget—killing yourself isn't going to help. Unless, you know, you really *do* want to kill yourself. In which case, there are a few ways that are a little more effective."

"Yeah, sure." Harland took another swig of the sports drink, not quite as deep as the first. He expected Aaron to skate away, to go do whatever it was he had come here to do, but the man just stood there, watching him.

His dark gaze was too intense, his rugged face too impassive. Harland couldn't tell what he was thinking and the experience was unnerving. He finally capped the drink and looked away. "I, uh, I'll clean this shit up and get out of your way—"

"No need. I can use the pucks." Aaron flipped the stick so the end was planted on the ice. He draped his arm across the blade, not quite leaning on it. "Unless you want to stick around and shoot some passes to me."

"Oh. Um—"

"No big deal. You probably have some place else to go."

"Actually, I don't." Wasn't that the truth? Yeah, he could go home but he didn't feel like dealing with his father's shit, especially not now. Hell, he'd never wanted to deal with his father. Ever. That was about the only thing in his life that hadn't changed.

Aaron watched him for a few long seconds, that dark gaze still too intense. Then he finally nodded, a small grin teasing the corner of his mouth. The scar that ran from his mouth to his chin deepened, making the grin oddly crooked and off somehow—and not necessarily in a good way.

Harland tossed the bottle to the side, watched as it slid into the boards. Then he moved around the ice, gathering the pucks into a pile. "Let me know when you're ready."

"I'm ready. Just start passing when you feel like it."

Harland nodded then pulled the first puck in with his blade. He pulled back with his stick and shot it forward, aiming it toward Aaron. It was an easy shot, almost too slow. The other man spun around, caught it, sent it flying into the net with a satisfying *whoosh*.

"I might be old, Day-glo, but I'm not dead. You don't need to take it easy on me."

Harland clenched his jaw at the nickname but didn't say anything, not when that would only make it worse. He grabbed another puck and sent it flying toward Aaron, a little harder this time.

Once more, the older man shot it into the net.

They kept it up for a half-hour, passing and shooting, back and forth. Nearly every single puck made it into the net, no matter how difficult Harland tried to make the pass. And then they switched so Aaron was the one making the passes. Harland didn't have the other man's luck when it came to getting the puck between the pipes.

"You're too fucking tense. You stiffen up damn near every time your stick touches the puck."

"Tell me something I don't know."

"So what the hell is going on? I watched you play last year, before you started fucking up. What happened?"

"Nothing." Harland turned his back on the other man and started collecting pucks, shooting them all toward the boards.

"Yeah, sure. Something happened. Your game doesn't tank like yours for no reason at all."

"It's nothing. I don't feel like talking about it."

"Suit yourself." Aaron leaned against the boards, his dark gaze following Harland's every move. "So if you don't want to talk about what happened then, how about what's going on now?"

"I don't know what you're talking about."

"Sure you do. Anyone with an eye can tell something else happened this past week. You're too fucking tense, irritable. And you're acting like the world just collapsed on top of you."

Harland slid to a stop and glared at the other man. "What are you, a fucking shrink?"

"No. But I'm a bit older, maybe I can help. If you want to talk, I mean. Or you can just keep driving yourself into the ground until you end up on the bench—or permanently scratched until your contract is up."

Fuck. Had he been that bad? Harland didn't think so but what the hell did he know? Obviously nothing. He had been driving himself, pushing over and over, but it seemed that the harder he pushed, the worse he got. He had thought—hoped—it was just his imagination.

Yeah, apparently not. And he couldn't afford to keep spiraling downhill, not with the regular season getting ready to start.

He looked away and ran a hand through his sweat-dampened hair, his mind racing. Should he talk to Aaron? Why the fuck would he? He didn't really know the other guy, hadn't really had any conversations with him until today. It wasn't like he could just blurt out everything that was going on, every worry and failure and uncertainty that was now plaguing him.

"Do you have kids?" The question came out of his mouth before he even realized he was going to ask it. Aaron stiffened for just a second, a frown creasing his rugged face.

"Yeah. Two. Why?"

"Is it—" Harland stopped, shook his head, not sure exactly what he wanted to ask. "I mean, how do you deal with it?"

"Deal with what?"

"Everything. I mean, life changes when you have kids, right? They come first. Nothing stays the same. I mean, that's how it's supposed to be, right? But what if you fuck things up instead?"

"Sorry, I'm the wrong one to ask."

"But you said—"

"Yeah, I know what I said. You're still asking the wrong guy. I haven't seen my kids for more than a week at a time in over two years."

"Oh." Well fuck. He'd really done it this time. Harland could feel his face heating up and he looked away, hoping Aaron would think it was from the exertion. "Sorry. I didn't mean to—"

"Yeah. No problem." Aaron shifted his weight from one skate to the other, his head tilted the side, his face expressionless. "My wife and I divorced a few years ago. She took the kids and moved back to Utah with her parents. It's, uh, complicated."

"Yeah. Sorry, man."

Aaron's face relaxed and he shrugged. "It is what it is. So why so curious about kids now? Thinking about having one? Or did you knock up one of those bunnies always hanging around?"

"No. Uh, nothing like that." Harland glanced down at

the stick in his hand, noticed how white his knuckles were, how numb his fingers were. He should have left his fucking gloves on, then maybe the stick wouldn't be in danger of breaking. He sucked in a deep breath and let it out slowly, easing his grip on the stick. "I just found out that, uh, my old girlfriend had a kid."

"Is she saying it's yours?"

"The opposite, actually. At least tried to. But he's definitely mine. His name is Noah and he's—" Harland paused, frowning as the realization hit him. Fuck, he didn't even know how old his own son was. He did the math in his head, trying to remember. It had been early October when Courtney told him she was pregnant—he remembered that much because the season was just getting ready to start. And that had been three years ago. Three long years that had changed everything.

Harland glanced over at Aaron and wondered if he noticed the pause. "He's almost three."

A ghost of a smile hovered around the other man's mouth. "That's a good age. They really start getting into everything and learn how to test your patience."

"I've, uh, only seen him once."

"Oh." Aaron shifted his weight again then ran one large hand over his mouth. His eyes seemed to drift out of focus, like he was seeing something that wasn't there. Maybe he was because he gave himself a shake then fixed those dark eyes on Harland. "So what are you going to do?"

"I don't know."

"Maybe I should rephrase that. What do you *want* to do?"

"About what?"

"Listen, you brought this up for a reason. The way I see it, you only have two choices: you either claim him as yours and become part of his life, or you keep going on like you did before you even knew about him and stay out of his life."

The words were nothing more than a harsh echo of his own mind's ramblings. Hadn't that been exactly what he was thinking? Exactly what he was struggling with? Maybe his mind had phrased them a little differently but the meaning stayed the same.

But hearing them spoken out loud didn't help with his struggles, his fears. He risked another glance at Aaron but the man wasn't watching him. "I don't know anything about being a father."

"Shit. You think it comes with a fucking handbook? You just do the best you can for them based on what you know and hope you don't totally fuck things up."

"Yeah, well." Harland ran his thumb along the edge of blade, picking at the worn tape. "My father wasn't—isn't—exactly a good example. I don't have shit to go on, you know?"

"First, you have to ask yourself what you want to do. If you decide to keep things the way they were before you found out, then you're worrying over nothing." Aaron tossed his stick onto the bench then grabbed the bucket by his feet. "If you decide you want to be in the kid's life, then you just do the things your old man didn't do. Or don't do what he did. Either-or. Learn from his mistakes and try not to repeat them."

"Is that what you did?"

"I'm not exactly the right one to ask. My kids are with their mother, remember?" Aaron turned away and busied himself with picking up the pucks scattered around them. Harland didn't miss the flash of regret and pain in the other man's eyes, though, and he mentally kicked himself for asking. But he had one more question he needed to know, one more question he had to ask.

"What about you? If you could go back and do things differently, would you just, you know, choose not to have them?" And fuck, could the question have come out any more wrong than it did? Aaron spun around, his eyebrows lowered in an angry slash over heated eyes. Harland half-expected the other man to take a swing at him. He wouldn't duck, wouldn't avoid it, figuring that was the least he deserved.

But Aaron didn't take a swing, didn't lunge, didn't flinch. He just watched Harland with those dark intense eyes for a long minute, his face carefully blank. And when he spoke, his voice was filled with regret—and with a fiery emotion Harland didn't quite understand.

"What would I have done? I would have fought my ex. Hard. With everything I had. I would have kept fighting until there was nothing left. And after there was nothing left, I still wouldn't have stopped fighting."

CHAPTER EIGHT

Courtney gathered up the empty bottles and tubes of color and tossed them in the trash, then peeled the gloves from her hands. A little soap and water, a little lotion, and she was ready for her next client. Her eyes drifted to the clock on the wall beside her. Not quite time for the next appointment, which meant she could finally take her break and relax.

Well, maybe not *relax*. She hadn't been able to relax for a few weeks, not since Harland had barged back into her life and sent her world spinning. Harland's intrusion had been bad enough, with all the phone calls and banging on the door that first week. That had stopped, filling her with an odd sense of something that should have been relief but wasn't.

And then the calls from the attorney started. At least once a day, until they had finally just unplugged the phone. There had been a few letters, too, but those had gone promptly in the trash. Courtney didn't want to look at them, couldn't bear to see what they might say. If she didn't open them, didn't read them, they didn't exist.

Because it wasn't just her world anymore—it hadn't

been just her world since the day Noah was born. Harland had no right to come storming back into it and turning everything upside down, not after everything he'd said.

She moved down the hall to the small breakroom, stopping in front of the tiny cubby that housed her bag and jacket. The aspirin she was searching for wouldn't do anything to alleviate the knot of tension she had been carrying between her shoulder blades but it might help the headache. Right now, she'd take all the help she could get.

"You're going to give yourself an ulcer if you keep taking those. They're not good for your stomach, you know that."

She looked over her shoulder and gave Beth a small smile, then shook out three of the plain white pills. "What makes you think I don't already have an ulcer?"

"It wouldn't surprise me, as tense and jumpy as you've been. Are you ever going to tell me what's going on?"

"Nothing's going on."

Beth snorted, the sound entirely too delicate to carry as much sarcasm as it did. Her friend stepped behind her and placed her small hands on Courtney's shoulders, her fingers digging in to the knotted muscles. "Damn, girl. You're tighter than my last boyfriend's ass."

Courtney's eyes drifted closed and her head dropped forward. "Which boyfriend was that?"

"The firefighter."

"Adam?" Courtney raised her head, only to have Beth push it back down. "I thought you liked him."

"I did. But he lives too far away. That, and he started looking for more than a booty call. I wasn't interested." She heaved a dramatic sigh. "But damn, I will miss that ass. And everything else he had to offer."

Courtney laughed, surprised at how foreign it felt. Beth yanked the end of her hair and tugged her over to the small table. "Sit down if you want me to keep rubbing. You're too tall for me to do this with you standing up."

"I am not tall."

"Okay, I'm short. I said it. Are you happy?"

Courtney laughed again and settled into the hard chair, leaning forward so Beth could continue working the knots from her back. "I really thought you and Adam were going to be a thing. Don't you ever want to settle down?"

"Who, me? Nah. I'm allergic to commitment, you know that." Beth pushed against one stubborn knot, causing Courtney to hiss and hunch her shoulders. "Sorry. What about you? Don't you ever want to take a break from your self-imposed celibacy?"

"Beth! You did not just say that!"

"Sure I did. I mean, seriously. When's the last time you went out on a date?"

"I'm a single mom, it's not that easy."

"Sure it is. A guy asks you out, you say yes. Simple as that."

"No, I can't. I have Noah. You know that. And you also know that no guy would be interested in seeing a twenty-one-year-old single mother of a child with Noah's issues."

"I think you just use that as an excuse because you don't *want* to go out."

Courtney ignored the comment, knowing what would happen if she answered. They'd had this conversation before—too many times. Beth would try to fix her up with someone, try to talk her into going out. Courtney always said no. That wasn't her life right now. It had never been her life.

"So you never did tell me how you and the hot firefighter met."

"Trying to change the subject, hm? Fine, I won't bring up your serious lack of a social life again. For now. And I'm seriously not telling you how we met."

"Why not?"

"Because it might offend your virginal sensibilities, that's why."

"I am hardly virginal. I have a kid, remember?"

Beth laughed, the short sound holding a world of sarcasm and disbelief. "Okay. So you had sex. Once. Over three years ago. I'm so impressed."

Courtney opened her mouth to disagree, to tell Beth she'd had sex more than once. A *lot* more than once. She snapped her mouth closed and swallowed the words. Saying them out loud would take this entire conversation down a different road, one she didn't want to travel. One she didn't want to remember.

So she didn't date. So what? Her priority was Noah. Life now wasn't always easy but she didn't regret her choices, not for one minute. And if she sometimes felt overwhelmed...well, what mother didn't? She had her own mother to help out. And friends like Beth. And she had her son. That was all she needed.

"No comeback, hm?"

"I know better."

Beth murmured something, her hands working magic on the tense muscles. Courtney leaned forward even more, releasing her breath and letting herself relax. The music piped into the salon's speakers was muted back here, nothing more than a backdrop for the other sounds surrounding them. The chatter of conversation between stylist and client was nothing more than a relaxing buzz, lulling her deeper into a foggy gray world. The phone rang from somewhere out on the floor; the bell signaling the arrival or departure of another client was nothing more than a barely-heard tinkle.

In a few minutes, she'd have to get back up. Go to work with her next client, shampooing and cutting. But for now, for these few precious minutes, she could try to relax and distance herself from life.

"Your purple is fading."

"Hm?"

"I said your purple is fading." Beth's hands moved to her hair and separated out a thick strand. "You should change it."

PLAYING THE GAME

Courtney sighed and straightened, reaching back to pull her hair from Beth's hand. "I happen to like the purple."

"I know you do. But Fall's here. New season, new color. I'm thinking you'd look really good with some red."

"Red? I don't think so—"

"Not *red* red. More like an auburn cinnamon. With highlights. That would really make your color pop."

"What's wrong with my color?"

"Nothing. Except you've been so stressed lately that you're super pale. The blonde only makes you look more washed out."

"Oh, and going red would be any better?"

"Sure. A nice warm color, nothing too drastic." Beth started running her fingers through her hair, pulling strands in different directions. "We've never done a red on you before. I think it'll look good."

"I don't know. Maybe."

"No maybes about it. I already know what I'm going to do. Can you stay late tonight? I'll do it then—"

"Hey Courtney, someone's here to see you."

Courtney glanced at the clock then turned toward Shelly, another stylist. There was something about the other woman's expression that made Courtney's hands curl into fists. This wasn't about her next client—or any client, for that matter. Courtney knew that with a certainty that froze her.

A man stood behind Shelly, middle-aged in a dark nondescript suit. Everything about him was nondescript. Average, unassuming. Someone you'd pass on the street and not even notice.

So why did he fill Courtney with so much fear? And why did Beth suddenly place a hand on her shoulder, like she was offering support?

"Miss Williams?"

"Y-yes?"

The man pushed past Shelly, a white envelope held in his hand. He stopped in front of her, his face blank of all expression, and held the envelope out to her. "This is a request for a paternity test on one Noah Robert Williams. The information on where to have the test taken is inside. I would suggest you not ignore it."

"What?" The word came out as a strangled whisper. She could have screamed it and the man wouldn't have cared: he was already walking out. Beth's hand tightened on her shoulder and she leaned closer, peering at the envelope in Courtney's shaking hand.

Courtney looked down at it, the black lettering swimming in front of her. She squeezed her eyes closed, opened them, blinked until the lettering came into focus. Her stomach clenched when she recognized the return address. It was the same law firm that had sent the other letters she had thrown away.

"Courtney! Oh my God. What is it? Open it! What did he mean? Paternity? For Noah? Why? For what?" Beth's questions came one after the other, the words nothing more than senseless sound, lost in the sudden buzzing surrounding Courtney.

She dropped the envelope onto the table and pushed her chair back, nearly knocking Beth over. "Throw it in the trash. I don't want it."

"Shelly, grab me a bottle of water." Beth bent down next to her and placed a comforting hand on her leg. Her other hand snagged the envelope from the table and held it between them. "Courtney, I don't think you can ignore this. You heard him. You need to open it."

"No. No, I don't."

"Courtney, he sounded serious. You need to open it."

"I can't."

"You have to. But I don't understand, why would anyone want a paternity test on Noah? I thought you said you knew who his father was."

"I did. I do." And oh God, why was he doing this? It was Harland, it had to be. Of course it was him. But why? What he was hoping to prove?

Or was he trying to prove Noah wasn't his? Was that what this was about? No, it couldn't be. There was no reason for him to do that. She didn't want anything from him, wouldn't even think of asking him for anything. And Harland hadn't even known about Noah until he barged back into their lives a month ago. He would have *never* known. So why?

She shifted in the chair, her frantic gaze resting on Beth. "Open it for me. I can't. I don't want—you have to open it."

Beth watched her for a long minute, a hundred different unasked questions flashing through her hazel eyes. Then she nodded and slowly opened the envelope, her fingers shaking. She pulled out a single sheet of paper, the letterhead matching what was on the envelope.

Beth looked at her once more, silently asking permission to read it. Courtney nodded, watched as Beth's eyes skimmed the several short paragraphs.

"What does it say?"

"It's a bunch of legal jargon." Beth frowned, her eyes skimming the page once more. "Something about something called an Acknowledgement of Paternity to establish—ohmygod. I know this name. Holy shit. Oh. My. God. Courtney! Seriously? *He's* Noah's father? Holy shit, I don't believe it."

Courtney snatched the paper from Beth's shaking hand and read it for herself. The words didn't make sense, not really, not until after the third time. Even then, she wasn't entirely sure what every word meant. But she understood the general meaning.

Harland wanted to establish his paternity in order to file a correction to Noah's birth certificate so it would list him as the father.

But why? Why did it matter to Harland? Why would he go to the trouble and expense of hiring an attorney? He wasn't in Noah's life. She didn't *want* him in Noah's life.

"Is he really Noah's father?"

Courtney folded the letter and carefully tucked it back into the envelope, unable to look at Beth. "Yes."

"You? And Harland Day? But—"

"It was a long time ago, okay? I don't like thinking about it."

"How can you *not* think about it? He's Noah's father!"

"And he didn't even know about Noah until a few weeks ago! I don't know why he's doing this. It makes no sense—"

"But isn't this a good thing? I mean, it looks like he *wants* to be named as Noah's father. That means you can get him to pay child support and help—"

"No!" Courtney jumped from the chair and started pacing around the small room, her arms wrapped tightly around her middle. They had an audience now: Shelly and Diane and Jackie crowded together in the doorway, their expressions ranging from concern to blatant curiosity. Courtney didn't care. She was too upset to care.

She paused her frantic pacing, glanced at the women huddled in the doorway, then turned back to Beth. "I don't want his money. I don't want his help. I don't want anything to do with him and I don't want him in our lives."

"But why? Wouldn't this help—"

"Because he accused me of sleeping with someone else when I first told him I was pregnant. He kept insisting, over and over and over, that it wasn't his. That it couldn't be his." Courtney made an angry swipe at her cheek, not surprised that her hand came away damp. "So I told him it wasn't. I told him I wouldn't have it and that was it. I never saw him again."

"Oh, Courtney." Beth hurried over to her and pulled her into a comforting hug. Several more pairs of arms joined them, offering words of comfort and consolation and support. Courtney didn't know how long they stood there, huddled together. Beth was the first one to pull away. She wiped her own face, her mouth trembling with a watery smile.

"Okay, no more of this. Shelly, you and the others get back out there. Diane, can you take Courtney's next appointment?"

"Sure, no problem."

"I can take my own appointment." Courtney tried to object but Beth waved her off before shooing everyone out of the room. "Beth, I can take—"

"No, you can't." She grabbed the envelope from the table and held it out. "You need to get this taken care of first."

Courtney stepped back and shook her head. "No. I want nothing to do with that."

"Courtney, you can't ignore it."

"I'm not letting them put more needles in Noah. I'm not. Not for this. I don't care what they say."

"Then go talk to his father."

"Beth, I told you, I don't want—"

"This isn't going to go away, no matter how much you want it to. You should at least go talk to him. Maybe there's another way. Maybe there's some way to work this out so you're *both* happy."

Happy? That would never happen, not the way Beth meant. But maybe there was something else she could do, some way to talk Harland out of this insanity. She stared down at the envelope in Beth's outstretched hand, eyeing it with distaste and fear.

Then she reluctantly took it, surprised that it didn't weigh more than it did. It was just a letter. A simple letter in a plain envelope. But it had the potential of completely destroying the world as she knew it. Shouldn't it weigh more than it did?

She tightened her hand around the letter, not caring that she was crumpling it. Then she raised her eyes and looked at Beth. "I don't know what to do."

"Go talk to him. It's the only thing you *can* do for now."

CHAPTER NINE

Harland lowered the volume on the television and cocked his head, listening. Had someone knocked at the door? No, he must be hearing things. Besides, there was a doorbell right there in plain sight. If anyone was outside the door, they'd ring the bell, not knock.

He grabbed the remote, ready to edge the volume back up, when he heard it again. It wasn't even really a knock, more like a light tap.

"What the fuck?" Impatience edged his voice. He jabbed the remote with one finger, pausing the video of the game he'd been studying, then pushed off the sofa. Maybe he was hearing things. Or maybe it was just some kids playing games. If that was the case, he was going to let them have it. He wasn't in the mood for games. Hell, he wasn't in the mood for people, period. That was why he had backed out on meeting Jason and Zach later, and why he'd told his father to get lost for a few hours.

He yanked the door open, ready to read the riot act to whatever unfortunate soul happened to be standing there. Every scathing word died in his throat, replaced by nothing more than a gasp that came out as a wheeze.

Courtney stood in the hallway, her arms wrapped tightly around her middle. She was dressed in form-hugging black pants, a jacket at least a full-size too big for her hanging off her slim frame. An expression of pain distorted the fine features of her pale face. She'd been crying, he could tell from the smudged makeup around her eyes and the faint streaks on her face. His own heart lodged in his throat.

"Did something happen to Noah? Is he okay?" His voice shook, sounding strained to his own ears. She didn't say anything, just stood there, staring at him. He reached for her arm, ready to pull her inside, to pull her into his arms. His hand barely grazed her when she pulled away, stepping out of his reach with a small moan of despair.

"Why? Why would you do this?"

"Do what? Courtney, what's wrong? What happened?"

"This!" She pulled an envelope from her jacket and waved it in front of his face, so fast he could barely make out what it was. But he didn't need to see it—he knew what it was.

The concern—the fright—that had shaken him only seconds before disappeared in the space of a heartbeat. Anger and impatience took their places. He leaned against the doorframe, no longer worried about inviting her inside, and stared at her through narrowed eyes.

"You finally got it, huh?"

"Why, Harland? What is this about? Why would you do this to me?"

"To *you*? Honey, this has nothing to do with you. Noah's my son. I want that on record."

"But why? I don't understand."

"You don't need to understand, now do you? This has nothing to do with you."

"It has everything to do with me. Noah is *my* son. I'm not going to let you put him through this."

Harland leaned forward, his anger growing. "He's my son, too. You seem to keep forgetting that."

"You didn't want him! You didn't want anything to do with him! You didn't even want to hear that he was yours when I told you I was pregnant." Her voice was a plaintive wail, the final words dying amid choking tears. He watched as she tried to stop them, as she brushed one hand across her face.

The muscle in his jaw jumped as he clenched his teeth. He tried to tamp down his own emotions, tried not to let the sight of Courtney crying get to him.

Tried...and failed. Because no matter what everyone thought of him, no matter how hard and cold he pretended to be, he wasn't the heartless bastard everyone thought he was.

Harland reached for her again, surprised she didn't struggle to rip her arm from his grasp. He led her inside and steered her toward the sofa, urging her to sit. Then he moved to the kitchen and ripped several sheets of paper towels from the roll before returning to the living room.

He sat down next to her, his leg brushing against hers. His body stiffened and he slid away, ignoring the flare of heat from just that small touch. What the fuck was wrong with him? Seriously? She was falling apart in front of him and he was wondering about getting closer to her?

He shoved the paper towels toward her then slid back a few more inches, wondering if maybe he should move to the chair. Because yeah, apparently he really *was* a heartless bastard because his body was still reacting to that small touch.

Courtney wiped a towel across her face, dragged it under her eyes then blew her nose. She looked like hell: worn out, tired, stressed. Her face was too pale, her eyes too wide, rimmed in red. Her normally full lips were nearly colorless, pressed together in a tight line. And her hands were shaking. He could see that without even really looking. Just like he could see she was trying to hide it by curling her fists around the wad of towels.

He looked away, ashamed of himself. Ashamed for

noticing her weakness, like he was somehow spying on her. Ashamed that he was partly to blame. Partly? Who the fuck was he kidding? He was the *only* one to blame. And he was going to make it worse. There was no doubt in his mind about that, no matter how much shame he felt.

Noah was his son, and he wasn't backing down from this.

"Why, Harland? I don't understand."

He shifted on the sofa, turning so he faced her. "He's my son."

"You keep saying that but he's not. You weren't there when he was born. You've never been there. You didn't even know about him! So why? Why does it matter? Why now?"

"Because I *do* know about him. And I'm not going to walk away."

"Please don't do this to him. To me."

"Do what? You're acting like this is such a big deal. I'm his father. I *want* to be in his life. Why are you fighting me on this?"

"Because you're going to walk away again. Just like you did last time. I know it." The words were barely more than a whisper but she might as well have shouted them for the effect they had on him. He felt like he'd been punched, hard, then slammed into the boards. The pain was a physical thing, shoving the breath from his lungs and leaving him feeling battered.

It wasn't just the words. It was the look in Courtney's wide brown eyes: flat, distant...and filled with complete certainty. She wasn't worried he *might* walk away—she was convinced that was exactly what he'd do.

He wanted to argue with her, tell her she was wrong. But he couldn't. How could he, when it was exactly what he'd done three years ago? He wanted to tell her he wasn't the same person he had been back then.

Another truth. Except was the person he was now any better? Harland clenched his jaw and looked away. He couldn't answer that question. No, that wasn't right. He didn't *want* to answer that question—because he was truly afraid of the answer.

That didn't mean he was going to back down or give up. Not even close. This was too important.

He relaxed his jaw, forced his hands to unclench, then turned back to face Courtney. "I'm not backing down on this."

Maybe she heard the finality in his voice, or saw something in his eyes. Her color paled even more and she leaned forward, her slender hand wrapping around his wrist, squeezing.

"Please don't do this, Harland. You don't know what Noah's been through. All the tests, the needles, the exams. He's just now gotten to the point where I can get him into the doctor's without him throwing a fit." The words caught and hitched in her throat. Harland felt a corresponding hitch in his own chest.

Courtney's hand tightened around his wrist, her eyes softening—almost begging—as she leaned even closer. He caught the faintest whiff of her perfume, something too light to define. Tell-tale moisture appeared in her eyes and she blinked it away. Her lips parted and for one second of pure insanity, he thought about what it would be like to kiss her again. Would her lips be as soft and welcoming as before? Would his body heat and clench with desire from just one kiss?

And fuck, he really was a bastard. His body was already reacting to her nearness, his cock growing hard at just the memory of her body against his. He pulled his gaze away from hers, forced himself to focus on her words.

On the pleading desperation of her voice.

"Please Harland. I'm begging you. Don't make me put him through this. I'll do anything."

"Anything?" The question was out before he knew he was going to say it. Her eyes widened and he saw a flash of something in her eyes. Anger? Hurt? Certain knowledge that he was, indeed, a bastard of the worst kind? Because he knew exactly what she was thinking, knew exactly what she expected him to say, to ask for.

She pulled back but didn't release the hold she had on his wrist. Coldness replaced the anger in her eyes but she didn't look away. "Yes. Anything."

He wanted to take her up on it. To test her resolve and see if she really meant it. The temptation was strong, almost overwhelming. One kiss. One touch. One hour with her body.

No, more than one hour. A night. One night.

And even that wouldn't be enough.

The realization blindsided him, nearly knocking the breath from his lungs. He still wanted her. After everything that happened between them, after the pain and betrayal of the past—and the pain to come in the future—he still wanted her.

Needed her.

Could he do it? Could he take her up on the unspoken answer? Yeah, he could. He wanted to do. But he wouldn't. If he did, he'd only prove himself to be what she thought he was. And suddenly, that wasn't enough. Not nearly enough.

More than he wanted her, he wanted to prove she was wrong. Not just to her, but to himself. He'd been the arrogant bastard for too long and it had gotten him nowhere. He wasn't going to play that game anymore, not when there was so much more at stake.

He eased his hand from her grip and moved away from her, putting distance between them. Surprise flashed in her eyes, surprise that mimicked his own.

"We don't need the blood test for the Acknowledgement of Paternity if you agree to sign the paperwork."

Courtney made no move to hide her surprise—or her confusion. "The paperwork?"

"Yes. My attorney already has everything drawn up. We

both just need to sign it and he'll handle submitting it."

"But...I don't understand. Submitting it for what?"

"To correct Noah's birth certificate so it lists me as the father." She opened her mouth but Harland shook his head, cutting her off. "It's going to happen, Courtney. You can either agree to this, or the next step is a court order. And don't think I won't push for that because I will."

A dozen different emotions swirled through her eyes, ranging from confusion and disbelief to contempt and disdain. He could see the silent question beneath them all, the same question she had been asking since he opened the door: Why? He expected her to ask again, but she didn't.

And he was grateful for that, because it wasn't a question he could easily answer. He didn't know why; at least, not in a way he could put into words, not so she could understand. This was something he wanted to do. Something he *needed* to do.

She sat back, curling into herself as she huddled into the corner of the sofa. Silence hung between them, thick with uncertainty and accusation. Harland watched her, looking for any sign of further fight—looking for any sign of emotion besides the contempt burning clear in her damp eyes. But there wasn't any, certainly nothing even close to resembling the painful revelation that had gripped him moments ago.

She finally looked away, slowly nodding her agreement. The motion caused several thick strands of hair, a mix of pale blonde and purple, to fall into her face. He wanted to push them away, wanted to see her face.

Because suddenly her agreement wasn't enough. He wanted more than just his name on a piece of paper, needed her to realize he was serious about that.

"I'll have my lawyer set up the appointment."

She nodded again and shifted, ready to stand. No doubt ready to run from him as she called him every foul name that she could think of. His next words stopped her.

"That's not all. I want to see him. Spend time with him. Get to know him and let him get to know me."

Her head twisted around, anger flashing in her eyes. "You can't—"

"Yes, I can. And I will. Don't doubt me on this, Courtney."

"I don't want you to! Don't you understand that? I don't want you to have anything to do with Noah. I don't want you in our lives."

"I know you don't. But unless you feel like fighting me on this, I don't think you have any choice. And there will be a fight. All I have to do is call my attorney."

She pushed off the sofa, each motion short and clipped, filled with the rage he could feel rolling off her. Her steps faltered and she stumbled, righted herself before she reached the door. Then she turned, her eyes blazing in spite of the tears building in them.

"I hate you."

Harland didn't let her see him flinch, couldn't let her know how deeply the words cut. "I know."

CHAPTER TEN

Harland glanced up at the scoreboard, watching the replay. So fucking close. Just an inch to the left and the fucking puck would have gone in.

Fuck.

Someone tapped him on the back and he turned, surprised to see Bryan Torresi, their head coach, nodding at him. No, he hadn't scored, but at least the coach wasn't throwing shit behind the bench. That had to be a good sign, right?

Just the fact that he was playing was a good sign.

His game still sucked. He still couldn't find the fucking net. But he wasn't scratched, and he was actually getting some ice time. Nowhere near as much as he used to, but more than he had the end of last season.

More good signs.

But he wished the fucking puck would have gone into the net.

He reached for one of the water bottles and shot a stream into his mouth, swishing it around before leaning to the side and spitting it out. He shot another stream into his mouth and swallowed, his eyes searching the sparse crowd seated around the arena.

Why the fuck hadn't he scored? He'd wanted it so damn bad, more than he'd wanted it in a long time. Noah was out there somewhere, watching him. Against Courtney's will but she didn't have much choice, not when Harland insisted she bring him. And maybe it was silly and totally foolish, but he'd wanted to score to make his son proud.

Except Noah didn't even know who he was. And he'd bet his fucking salary the kid didn't even know what the hell was going on. It didn't matter. He was here—that was what mattered.

"What the fuck are you doing?" Jason tapped him on the leg with his stick, a frown on his sweaty face.

"What?"

"I asked what the fuck you were doing. You're looking everywhere but the ice. Come on, man, get with it."

Harland grunted but didn't say anything. Jason was right, he needed to stop searching the crowds, needed to pay better attention. The score was tied with ten minutes left in the third. A lot could happen in those ten minutes.

He leaned forward, his arms braced on his knees as Aaron battled to win the faceoff. Yes! Aaron passed the puck behind him to Kyle Middleton, who moved up the ice. Back and forth: Kyle to Aaron to Zach. One of the goons from Rochester hurried toward Zach but Ben Leach was faster, getting there in time to stop the guy from taking him out.

Harland leaned forward, his eyes focused on the play unfolding in front of him. His teammates passed the puck in front of the net, getting into position. Kyle to Zach to Aaron. Everyone on the bench went still, collective breaths held as Aaron moved in closer, pulled his stick back—

Another Rochester player charged Aaron, catching him straight across the back. Aaron dropped to his knees as the puck went wild, careening behind the net. A whistle blew, sharp and long, ending the play.

"Day-glo, get out there for Aaron. You know what I want you to do." Coach Torresi's voice was brusque as he called out orders, expecting immediate compliance. Harland didn't hesitate, just jumped the boards and moved down ice to get into position.

"Fucking dirty play from your teammate there, fuck-wad. Guess that's the only way you douche canoes can win." Harland pitched the words low enough so only the guy from Rochester could hear. The guy looked at him, the sneer on his face clear, then turned and spit.

"Fuck you."

"Simple mother fucker. How long did it to take you to learn that comeback, asshole? Had to really tax the shit you have for brains for that one, didn't you? Fuck-wad."

Another sneer. Harland leaned forward, meeting the other man's gaze, then smiled. Wide, bright, and full of contempt. The guy's eyes narrowed and he started to say something just as the puck dropped. Harland barreled into him, pushing him out of the way to get into position.

Zach was in possession now, playing with the puck, his gaze darting between Harland and Kyle. He started to pass it to Kyle, stopped to spin around, shot it toward Harland.

He reached out with his stick, felt the puck hit the blade, moved back and to the left. Zach was in position to the side of the net, all Harland had to do was pass it—

Something hit him from behind with the force of a bulldozer, throwing him off balance. His shot went wild and he spun around, already throwing his stick and gloves to the ice. One punch caught him under the chin, making him see stars. His helmet flew off, landing somewhere behind him.

Another punch caught him just under the eye and he felt the sting of skin splitting. It didn't matter, not when he could do this with his eyes closed. He grabbed a handful of sweaty jersey with his left hand and let loose with his right, landing more punches than he received.

Rough hands grabbed him, pulling him back, separating

them and stopping the fight. Harland turned his head to the side and spit then tugged his jersey back into place. He grabbed his gear from the ice and headed over to the sin bin, pausing long enough to give the other guy another wide smile.

Maybe his scoring was still totally fucked up, but there was nothing wrong with his fighting.

CHAPTER ELEVEN

No, there was nothing wrong with his fighting.

Except the pain afterward, which Harland was feeling forty minutes later in the locker room. A butterfly bandage was in place, covering the cut below his eye. An icepack on his jaw had helped with the swelling, but there was nothing to do for the scrapes on his knuckles. Some antiseptic and a little ice and he was ready to go.

He glanced at his watch and swallowed back a groan when he saw how late it was. Courtney was supposed to meet him by the main doors of the concourse fifteen minutes ago. Would she still be there? Yes, she had to be. Harland didn't want to think of the alternative.

He shrugged into the suit jacket and adjusted his tie then grabbed the small duffel from the bench. He tossed it over his shoulder and turned, running straight into Jason and Zach.

"You going with us tonight?"

Harland frowned at Jason. "Going where?"

"Out." Zach motioned with his hands, a wide grin on his face. "You know, go have a few drinks, pick up some women. Celebrate the win. Out."

"No, I can't. I'm meeting someone." Harland glanced at his watch again and tried to tamp down his impatience. "And I'm already running late."

"Who are you meeting?"

"Yeah. And since when are you ever on a timeline?"

"Since I have someplace to be, that's since when. And it's none of your business." He tried to push past them, hoping they'd let it go and not ask any more questions. No such luck. They started walking with him, one on each side, the questions almost nonstop.

Harland pushed the up button on the elevator then turned back to face them. "Guys, leave it alone. It's not what you think. I'm just taking my son out for ice cream."

Jason and Zach both fell silent, identical expressions of shock on their faces. The elevator door opened behind him and Harland turned. Jason pushed in front of him, blocking his way.

"Whoa. Whoa, whoa, whoa. What the fuck did you say?"

"You heard me."

"No, I don't think we did." Zach moved in, crowding him from the other side. "Say that one more time, slowly."

Harland moved the bag from one hand to the other, no longer bothering to hide his impatience. "My son. Come on, guys, out of the way. I'm already late."

Zach grabbed his arm. "Wait. You can't just drop that bombshell and run away. When the fuck did you get a son?"

"Not now, guys." Harland pulled his arm from Zach's hold then pushed past Jason just as the elevator doors started to close. He half-expected them to jump in the elevator with him but they didn't.

"Tomorrow. After practice. You've got—" Jason's words were cut off by the closing door. Harland sagged against the wall and sighed in relief. He didn't need the two of them making this any more awkward than he was afraid it would already be. And he sure as hell didn't need either one of them around Courtney. That would be a fucking nightmare of epic proportions he didn't even want to consider.

The door opened and he stepped out into the empty concourse. Everything was closed, the food and drink vendors, the souvenir concessions. Wire gates were pulled down, lights turned off. Fuck, was it later than he realized? He resisted the urge to check his watch again and hurried along the wide hall, the soles of his dress shoes clicking with each step.

Would Courtney and Noah still be there? Please let them still be there...

He turned the corner and stopped, his lungs aching for breath. Funny, he didn't remember holding his breath at all. It didn't matter because Courtney was standing just inside the door, talking to one of the security guards as Noah ran in a clumsy circle around her. No, not really *around* her. He was toddling back and forth in a tight half-circle, his hand held securely in Courtney's, her arm being dragged from front to back to front again with each half-lap Noah made.

Nobody noticed him and he took an extra minute to gather himself, to straighten his tie and jacket sleeves, to run a shaking hand through his hair. And all the time, his gaze was on Courtney.

He didn't know why his heart seemed to speed up at the sight of her. She wasn't dressed to stand out, wasn't wearing anything designed to attract attention. A pair of worn jeans sporting frayed holes in the legs, the hems tucked into a pair of black leather boots that stopped at mid-calf. A dark green sweater fell to her hips, the material almost shapeless on her.

And her hair...her hair was completely different. Instead of pale blonde with a purple streak, her hair was now a warm vibrant reddish-brown. It hung loose around her shoulders, the gentle waves framing her face. He'd never seen her hair this color before. Growing up, it had been a light brown color. She'd started highlighting it her junior year in high school, playing with the color until it was mostly all blonde. He remembered teasing her about it, never understanding the need to change colors so often. And he'd always smile and tell her he liked the original brown, just to get a reaction from her.

But he hadn't been lying. While all the shades of blonde she had experimented with looked good on her, he'd always missed the brown. Maybe it had been nothing more than nostalgia, but it had been his favorite.

Until now.

And Christ, what the hell was he doing? Was he really standing there like an idiot, gawking over the color of her hair? Yes, he was. He must be more nervous than he realized if he was doing something so foolish. At least, that's what he told himself.

He took a deep breath and let it out, then moved toward them. Noah saw him first because he suddenly stopped his back-and-forth marching and hid behind Courtney's legs. She glanced down at him then followed his wide-eyed gaze. Harland didn't miss the slight tensing of her shoulders, the subtle tightening of her mouth.

Great. Two strikes and the evening hadn't even started yet.

He forced a small smile to his own mouth and kept walking, pretending not to notice Noah's sudden hiding or Courtney's not-so-subtle body language. The security guard nodded at him, waved at Noah, then turned and left.

Now it was just the three of them.

The silence that settled over them was eerie, a heavy presence in the deserted concourse. Harland adjusted his grip on the bag and cleared his throat. "Sorry I took so long."

His voice was too loud, almost booming in the awkward silence. His gaze moved from Courtney to Noah and back again. Courtney watched him for a few seconds, her gaze resting on the bandage under his eye. Then she shifted, turning so she was actually facing him. Or was the move designed to better shield Noah? Harland tamped down his irritation, determined to make this outing a fun one.

He unzipped the bag and plunged his hand inside, searching for the souvenir he'd bought earlier. His fingers brushed against something soft and he closed his hand around it, bringing it out with a hesitant smile. He looked at Courtney, not sure if he should ask her permission or not.

No. Noah was his son. He didn't need permission to give his son a gift.

He bent down and extended his arm toward Noah. The gift was nothing more than a stuffed plane, a cartoon rendition of an old bomber with a soft gray material for the body and strips of black felt for the propellers. *The York Bombers* was embroidered in black stitching on the side. It even had a face stitched on it, the expression a cross between a smile and a grimace. At least, that's what Harland thought it was supposed to be. He wasn't really sure. Hell, he was still trying to figure out how this thing even remotely resembled the team's logo.

Noah's gaze, wide and curious, fixed on him then moved to the stuffed plane in his hand. He took a hesitant step toward Harland then paused and looked up at his mother. He pointed with his free hand, his tiny fingers moving.

Harland watched as Courtney did something with her own hand, her two inside fingers folded under, the other three spread out. She moved her hand, palm angled down, back and forth twice. Stopped, repeated it.

Noah's face scrunched up in concentration as he tried to mimic whatever Courtney had done. After the third time, she smiled and closed her hand into a fist and moved it back and forth, her head nodding at the same time. She looked at Harland, her hesitation clear, and sighed.

She made the spread-finger motion with her hand once

more. "This is the sign for 'plane'." She released her hold on Noah and gave him a reassuring pat on his back. "Go ahead, sweetie, you can take it."

Noah gave her an uncertain look then stepped toward Harland. He hesitated, took another step, then grabbed the plane from Harland's hand and hurried back to Courtney, stepping behind her once more.

She bent down, put her hands on her hips, and gave Noah a stern look. Harland smothered a smile: he didn't need any help interpreting that look. "What do you say, young man?"

Noah grinned, ran back toward Harland, and made a sign like he was blowing him a kiss. Then he ran back to Courtney once more. This time, at least, he didn't seem to want to hide behind her as much.

"That means 'thank you'."

"Oh." Harland stood back up, ignoring the stiffness in his legs. "Does he, um, can he hear at all?"

"No, not really. Not enough to matter. He can sense vibrations, so if you stomp or if something has a particularly heavy bass line, he more or less feels it."

"Oh. I thought...well, when you talked to him, I just thought he could hear you."

"That's just mom-language. I think it's universal." A small smile played around her mouth, sending a shot of warmth surging through him. Could she tell? He didn't know, just tried to hide his disappointment when her smile faded.

Harland looked back at Noah. One small hand was clutching the plane, holding it tight against his small chest like a deformed shield. The other hand was attached to Courtney's leg—not in a death grip, but definitely not eager to let go, either. And Noah was still watching him, his light brown gaze both curious and wary.

"He didn't seem this shy the last time I saw him."

"He's only seen you once, Harland, and that was almost two months ago, in his own home, not in some strange place. And you look different now than you did then."

"Oh. The suit?"

"Not just the suit." She motioned toward his face. "The cut, the bandage. The bruise on your jaw."

What she said made sense. It didn't mean it had to sit well with him. He had convinced himself that Noah would remember him, that he'd slide into the role of fatherhood with no problems. No, maybe it hadn't been a realistic expectation, but what did he know? Nothing, apparently.

"So. Are you guys ready? Was there any place in particular you wanted to go?"

She shook her head. "Not really. But he needs to eat. And wherever we go, we can't stay long."

Harland clenched his jaw, tamping down the sudden spurt of anger. "Courtney, don't do this. You said today would be fine because it was an afternoon game. You said there was no time limit—"

"I know. There isn't. But Noah goes to bed at eight and he still needs a bath before then." She bent down and started putting a coat on Noah, moving the stuffed plane from one hand to the other so she could get his arms into the sleeves. She glanced over her shoulder, her face carefully blank. "It's later than I thought. I, uh, I forgot how long your games could take."

There was nothing he could say to that, not without looking like a total ass, so he just waited while she bundled Noah into his jacket then shrugged into hers. Should he take Noah's hand? No, he didn't want to push too much. And he didn't want to feel any disappointment if Noah shied away from his again. There'd be time for that later.

They took another elevator downstairs to the small parking garage, this one smaller and nowhere near as well-lit as what he had become used to in Baltimore's arena. The chill was sharper down here, a little more biting, and he no longer questioned Courtney's choice of coat for Noah.

"Did you get the car seat?"

"Yes." Harland led them through the garage to the SUV, unlocking it with the remote before they reached it. He opened the back passenger door and pointed. "I'm not sure if I got it in right. The woman at the store helped but you might want to check, just in case."

Courtney nodded. She made a sign to Noah then released his hand and climbed into the back seat, muttering under her breath as she tugged and pulled and twisted.

Something small and warm touched Harland's hand and he looked down, surprised to see Noah looking up at him with a lopsided grin. Then, very slowly, the little boy reached up with both arms, the plane still carefully clutched in one hand.

Harland didn't move. He *couldn't* move. He was afraid if he did, the spell would be broken, that he'd scare the kid. But Noah was insistent and kept reaching up, a small wheezy grunt spilling from his lips.

Harland looked at Courtney, wondering how pissed she'd get. But she was still busy with the new car seat and wasn't paying any attention to them. Well, why the hell should he care what she thought? Noah was his son. If he wanted to hold him—if Noah wanted him to pick him up—then he would.

He reached down and placed his hands under Noah's arms then lifted him up. Harland wasn't quite sure what to do next, though. He didn't need to be because Noah leaned forward and wrapped his arms around Harland's neck and dropped his head on his shoulder.

A lump formed in Harland's throat and an even bigger one lodged in his chest. It would be so easy to tighten his arms around the small body resting against him, to never let go. He couldn't do that. Hell, he was even afraid to move. What if he tightened his arms too much? What if he was holding him the wrong way? Would the kid break?

He didn't want to hurt Noah but he had no idea what he was doing. He felt small in his arms, his weight barely noticeable. Fragile. Delicate. Precious. The most precious thing in the world.

"Everything looks good. I can—"

Harland caught Courtney's gaze as she climbed out of the backseat. A flash of irritation lit her eyes then disappeared, leaving her gaze carefully blank. Hooded. Did he look as guilty as he felt? Ridiculous. There was nothing to feel guilty about. He hadn't done anything wrong. That didn't stop him from trying to explain, to come up with an excuse.

"He wanted up. I didn't mean to—he just kept raising his arms like he wanted me to pick him up and—"

"It's okay." Courtney cut him off, her voice softer than he expected it to be. Did she understand? Maybe she did. "But now you're going to have to get him into the seat. And trust me, that isn't going to be easy."

"What do you mean?"

She sighed then walked to the other side of the SUV and opened the door. "Watch his head climbing in. And just prepare yourself."

"Prepare myself? For what? It can't be that hard." As soon as he said the words and climbed into the back, he learned exactly what she meant. It was like someone had thrown a switch and the child in his arms suddenly became possessed. His body stiffened and his back arched as Harland tried to put him into the car seat. His arms flung out, swinging, refusing to be restrained. He kicked out with his legs then twisted from one side to the next, over and over. Every single time Harland thought he might have Noah in place, he arched his back and started flailing again.

He glanced over at Courtney, noticed that she was biting back a smile. "You're not much help."

"Sorry."

"Does he do this all the time?"

"Not all the time, no. But I had a feeling, the way he was hanging on to you, that he might."

"Oh." Harland swallowed back the disappointment at

the thought that maybe Noah hadn't wanted to be picked up for the reason he had thought. Stupid. What did it matter? It didn't.

Except the kid was still struggling, making it clear that he was *not* happy about being put in the seat. Courtney climbed up on the seat, on the other side of Noah, and tried to get one arm through the strap. She paused, made a quick motion with her hand, saying "No" at the same time.

Noah stared at her, his small eyes narrowed. He mimicked the sign, shaking his head back and forth. Then he arched his back once more and swung out with both arms. One hand—his empty one, because he was still somehow holding onto the stuffed plane—caught Courtney in the mouth. She made a small sound of muffled pain and pulled away, one hand covering her mouth, the other making that same sign again.

"Are you okay?"

"Yeah, fine. It was just an accident."

"I don't care if it was an accident or not. I've had enough of this. Show me that sign."

"What sign?"

"The one for 'no'. That's what you were telling him, right?"

Courtney nodded, the unasked question clear in her eyes. But she remained silent and showed him how to make the sign.

Harland watched closely then turned back to his formerly-angelic-but-now-possessed son. He placed his left hand in the middle of Noah's chest, holding him in place, and carefully—forcefully—made the sign as Courtney had showed him.

"No!" His voice was stern, with just an extra hint of volume. He repeated the sign and said it again: "No!"

Noah's eyes went wide with surprise and his body went limp, almost like he was too shocked to keep fighting. His gaze never wavered from Harland's as he slipped Noah's arms into the straps and snapped the buckle into place between his legs. Noah watched him for another few seconds then smiled and pulled the stuffed plane in front of him, busying himself with playing with it.

"I don't think I've ever seen him settle down so quickly before."

"Yeah?" Harland was helpless to stop the sense of warm accomplishment that spread through him. It didn't hurt that Courtney actually smiled at him, too. Just a small one, nothing more than a brief lifting of the corners of her mouth.

Who knew? Maybe this parenting thing wouldn't be so bad after all.

CHAPTER TWELVE

How the hell had it gotten to this point?

Courtney dried her soapy hands on one of the towels then sat back on her heels, trying to decide if this was a dream—or a nightmare.

Trying to decide which one would be worse.

Noah was splashing in the soapy water, getting as much on her and the floor as he was on himself. He kept bouncing up and down, making the soft strangled sounds that equated laughter for him. Each bounce created waves in the old tub, which sent each of the rubber boats rocking. And the rubber animals, and the rubber alphabet blocks. He had so many toys floating around him, it was a wonder there was room for him in the tub.

In other words, it was nothing more than normal bath time—except for the man kneeling on the floor next to her. His shirt sleeves were rolled up past each elbow, his hands dangling in the soapy water. Courtney watched him from the corner of her eye, just watching, not thinking. Fine hair, now dark with water, sprinkled his arms. The muscles of his forearms rippled each time his arms moved, which was pretty much non-stop because he was trying to catch Noah. He finally laughed and shook his head, dropping the washcloth into the tub.

"I give up. You're like an eel. A slippery little eel."

Noah couldn't hear him, Courtney knew that. But her son knew Harland was saying *something*, something to him, something funny. Noah made his grunting little laugh and bounced up and down again. A wave of water sloshed along the side of the tub, soaking the front of Harland's shirt before he could sit back.

Noah must have thought that was particularly funny because he did it again, using his hands to make even larger waves.

"Noah! No, stop." Courtney didn't bother wasting time to sign, just leaned forward, trying to grab him. Her hand caught his arm, slipped off. She tried again, with the same result.

Why was she even bothering? He was turning it into a game. She had learned how to pick her battles long ago, and this was one time where it was better to back off. If she did, it wouldn't be a game any longer.

She sat back on her heels one more time, wondering if she should share that wisdom with Harland. He was the one reaching for Noah now, only he was having worse luck than she did.

And she still wasn't sure how he had ended up *here*, kneeling on the old tile floor of the dated bathroom, helping her with Noah's bath.

They had gone to dinner at a chain restaurant not far from the arena where the Bombers played. Harland had insisted on driving them home, flat out refusing to let them take the bus. Courtney didn't argue with him, not when she was grateful for the ride. She didn't mind riding the bus herself—she did it almost every single day. But she wasn't a big fun of taking Noah with her, not if she didn't have to.

So she had accepted the ride, not thinking anything of it. And she hadn't made a big deal of it when Harland insisted on carrying a half-sleeping Noah inside. The entire situation made her uncomfortable—Harland, actually wanting to be part of Noah's life? It seemed surreal. Unbelievable. And part of her was still convinced that he would disappear once the novelty wore off.

There was more to being a father than simply having your name on a birth certificate but Harland had insisted. Insisted? No, it was more like threatened. She had given in, for reasons she still didn't quite understand. What did it matter if his name was listed? It didn't, not when being a father encompassed so much more.

Had she really thought that he'd let it go at that? Yeah, she had. It didn't matter that he insisted on this time with Noah—and not just tonight, either. Courtney had wanted to fight him on that, too, but she didn't know how. She'd talked to an attorney—a friend of Beth's, since she couldn't afford one of her own. He told her she could fight if she wanted to but that it would be better if she worked with Harland. He'd told her that if Harland pushed back, he'd probably win. Not only that, as Noah's father, he could potentially go after her for custody, even if it was only partial. He was Noah's father, he was making an effort.

She didn't feel like she had a choice. She didn't want to push, didn't want to lose. And she was secretly afraid that if she did push, Harland and his attorney would push for even more. Courtney couldn't bear to even think of what might happen then.

She couldn't do anything except wait and hope the novelty would wear off and that Harland would eventually disappear from their lives again. The thought left her unsettled, made her feel helpless—and more than a little afraid, because it wasn't just helplessness she was feeling. No, there was definitely more to it than that. Disappointment. Fear. Sadness at the idea of him disappearing once more.

And that scared her more than anything. She shouldn't

be feeling any of those things, not after everything that had happened between them.

"Um. Hey, Court? I, uh, I think something's wrong with the little guy."

"What?" The words startled her as much as the old nickname and she straightened, immediately alert as her gaze shot to Noah. He was standing still, slightly bent over, a look of concentration on his face as he held himself.

She jumped up and snagged him from the tub, dripping water on the floor as she carried him over to the plastic potty chair sitting near the regular toilet. She plopped him down then stood back, a wide smile on her face.

"Potty? Do you need to use the potty, Noah?" She made the sign for him: her right hand closed in a fist, her thumb between her index and middle fingers. "Potty?"

"What are you doing?"

She glanced over her shoulder and frowned. "What's it look like I'm doing? We're trying to get him potty trained."

"By having him *sit*?"

"How else would we do it?"

"Court, boys don't *sit* to take a piss."

"They do to poop."

"He was holding his dick. Since when does that mean *poop*?" Harland stood up and grabbed a towel, drying his arms and wiping at the front of his shirt. She ignored the way the material clung to his broad chest and focused on his choice of words instead.

"We don't say *dick*. Do you have to be so crass? He's not even three!" It didn't matter that Noah couldn't hear the word, she didn't want anyone using inappropriate language around him.

"Okay, sorry. What do you want me to call it? His pee-pee?"

"No. It's 'penis'." And oh God, did she just say that? To Harland? Yes, she did. And worse, her eyes had dropped to the front of his pants when she said it. She didn't know why, hadn't even realized she was going to drop her gaze. Heat filled her face. It was foolish to think he hadn't noticed, not when she saw the way his eyebrows quirked before she looked away.

"Fine. He was grabbing his *penis*. The boy needs to piss and boys don't do that sitting down. You need to teach him the right way to do it."

"Really? And just how am I supposed to do that? I'm not exactly equipped to demonstrate the proper technique, you know."

"No, you're not."

Courtney didn't miss the underlying warmth in Harland's voice, didn't miss the way his mouth curled up at the corner. She shook her head, felt her face grow even warmer. Why would he even say something like that? Should she respond? No. God no. That would make things even worse.

Harland moved toward her, that grin still in place. "Time to let the expert teach him."

"What are you doing?"

"I'm teaching my son how to piss like a man." He leaned down and pulled Noah from the small potty chair, then set him on his feet and turned him around so he was facing it. One hand reached for his belt, pulling the end loose from the buckle. "Okay, kid. This is how we do it."

"Harland! Don't you dare!"

He paused, his hand on the button of the dress pants. "What?"

"Did you forget I'm standing here?"

"Yeah? And?"

"You can't be serious." Oh God, he wasn't serious, was he? Did he actually plan to show Noah while she was standing *right there*? Her gaze met his and she saw the amusement flashing in the depths of those honey-colored eyes. Amusement and something else. Was he teasing her? Daring her? Damn him. She couldn't tell, wasn't sure she really wanted to know.

"I don't have anything to be embarrassed about."

Courtney opened her mouth, snapped it closed. Her mind was completely blank and she had no idea how to respond. Harland laughed, the sound too warm, too familiar. He stepped toward her, placed a large hand on her shoulder and steered her toward the door.

"Go. Leave us men in peace."

"What?"

"You heard me. It's time for some male bonding over the porcelain throne. Out you go."

"But you—"

"Or you can stay. Your choice. It's not like you haven't seen it before. And you already know it won't bother me."

"But I—" Courtney closed her mouth with an audible snap. Harland laughed again and nudged her out of the bathroom, gently closing the door in her face.

She'd just been kicked out of her own bathroom! This couldn't be happening. It really couldn't.

But it was. She heard Harland's low voice, the words too muffled to make out. Laughter. The sound of the toilet seat being raised. Another chuckle, followed by the strangled sound of Noah's laugh.

"Courtney? Is everything okay?"

She turned, noticed her mother standing at the top of the stairs behind her, a book in her hand. Had she been so dazed she hadn't even heard her mom coming up the steps? Obviously, because there she was.

"Is everything okay?" Her mom repeated the question, concern on her face.

Courtney nodded, shook her head. Nodded again. "Uh, yeah. I guess. Harland's showing Noah how to—" She stopped, looked back at the bathroom door, felt a sharp sadness sweep over her. "He's showing Noah how to use the toilet. Standing up."

Her voice broke for reasons she didn't understand. A brief smile spread across her mother's face then quickly disappeared. "Why are you upset, sweetheart? Isn't that a good thing?"

She should say yes. Yes, it was a good thing. Yes, Harland was getting to know his son. Yes, maybe it was a sign he was serious. But she couldn't say any of those things. So she just shook her head and pushed past her mother, practically running down the stairs. She hesitated then hurried through the kitchen and out the back door, out into the lonely, chilled night.

CHAPTER THIRTEEN

The back door opened and she heard the shuffle of one hesitant step. Her time for feeling sorry for herself had come to an end. Just as well. She didn't need to be sitting out here in the cold night air, having a pity-party for one. And she certainly didn't need more time to think, not when she couldn't make sense of all the dizzying thoughts swirling through her mind already.

"I'm getting ready to come in now, Mom. Just give me a minute."

"Uh, sorry. It's just me."

Courtney froze at the sound of Harland's hushed voice. She didn't bother turning around, couldn't even look at him. If she didn't, maybe he'd go back inside. Better yet, maybe he'd just leave. Was that asking for too much?

Apparently so because he stepped all the way outside. She heard him pull the door closed, heard the sound of his steps coming closer. She pulled her lower lip between her teeth and looked to her right, away from him.

Please don't sit down. Please don't sit down.

Her silent plea was ignored. He lowered himself to the bench next to her. Too close, because she could feel the heat of his leg near hers. Then something soft and warm draped around her shoulders, making her jump. She reached up with one hand, surprised to feel the comforting softness of a fleece blanket. She adjusted the blanket more fully around her shoulders then glanced at Harland.

His face was lost in the shadows, his expression unreadable. But she could feel him watching her, knew he was studying her.

"I thought you might be a little cold, sitting out here without your coat."

"Oh. Th-thank you."

"No problem." He looked away and shifted on the bench, stretching his long legs in front of him. He propped his elbows on the table behind him and tilted his head back. Courtney's breath caught in her throat as memories assailed her.

How many times had he sat just like that, on this same exact picnic table? He'd stare up at the sky and point out the different constellations to her. Some of them were the actual constellations but mostly it was just stuff he made up. Silly things, like Horace the Hockey Player and Winifred the Wimp. They would sit out here for hours, his arm draped around her shoulders, and just talk.

Talk about whatever happened that day. About what they would do tomorrow. About their plans and dreams for the future.

Courtney's throat thickened and she looked away. How long ago had that been? A lifetime ago, when they were both different people, before real life caught up to them.

"You okay?"

"Hm? Yeah. Fine." She pulled the blanket more tightly around her, hoping he hadn't noticed the husky thickness of her voice.

"He peed."

She glanced at him, careful not to meet his eyes. It didn't matter, he was still gazing up at the sky. "What?"

Harland turned his head, just enough so she could see

his crooked smile. "Noah peed. Standing up. The kid needs to work on his aim, though."

The sound she made couldn't really be called a laugh. It was more like a whimper, a choked mix of laughter and sorrow that she didn't quite understand. Harland turned toward her, one hand reaching out. He stopped, letting his hand drop into his lap before he actually touched her.

"Don't worry, he didn't make that big of a mess. And I cleaned it up, so…" His voice trailed off and he just sat there, watching her. She cleared her throat and looked away.

"Oh. Uh, thanks." *Thanks?* That was all she could think to say? It seemed so…inadequate. Forced. Nothing more than an empty word uttered to fill an awkward silence between two people who no longer knew each other.

The thought filled her with even more sorrow. What was going on with her tonight? Why all the sadness? Why the trip down memory lane, filled with memories more bitter than sweet? No, that wasn't true. The memories weren't bitter, not all of them. Just the ones at the end, when things had fallen apart.

"By the way, I like your hair."

Courtney was sure her mouth was hanging open. What was Harland up to? She glanced at him but he wasn't looking at her. He was bent over, his clasped hands hanging loosely between his legs.

She brought a hand up to her hair, fingering it self-consciously. "My hair?"

He turned his head and grinned. "Yeah. The color. I like it. I meant to tell you earlier."

He liked her hair? He actually *noticed* her hair? She hadn't even given it any thought and now he was sitting here, making it a point to tell her he liked it?

She looked away again, discomfort filling her as she muttered thanks.

They both sat there, mere inches separating them physically but a lifetime of distance between them in reality. She kept expecting him to get up and leave, kept waiting for him to get up and leave. Why was he still here? Noah was no doubt in bed, probably already asleep. There was no reason for Harland to still be here.

But he didn't move, didn't leave, didn't say anything. The silence stretched around them, broken only by the occasional sound of a car passing by out front, or the sound of a door closing a few houses down. And at some point, the silence was no longer uncomfortable, no longer strained or awkward.

And then Harland spoke again, his voice soft, too quiet and serious.

"I'm sorry."

Courtney stiffened again. She shook her head, tried to force a smile she didn't feel. "For the mess? You don't have to be. You cleaned it up, right?"

A large hand closed over her leg, its warmth almost scalding her. She stiffened even more, turned to find Harland watching her, his gaze too intense, focused solely on her. Her heart slammed into her chest and her lungs squeezed together, making it hard to breathe.

"Not for that, Courtney."

She wanted to look away, *needed* to look away. But his gaze held hers, as forcefully as if he was physically pinning her in place with his large body. She shook her head. In denial? But of what? Or was she merely begging him not to say anything else?

"I—" He stopped, his mouth pursed in a tight line. She could see his hesitation, *feel* his wariness. But he didn't look away. "The way I treated you. The things I said...you have every right to hate me."

"Harland, I—"

"Let me finish." He took a deep breath and finally looked away, glanced down at his hand, still resting on her leg. He moved it away, curled it into a fist and placed it on top of his own leg. "I was an ass. Worse than an ass. Hell, some people would say that hasn't changed. But I didn't mean—I should have never said what I did. I shouldn't have—"

"Harland, don't. Please." Her voice broke, her throat clogged with the same tears filling her eyes. She didn't want to hear him say these things, didn't want to relive those awful moments from that day three years ago.

He looked up, whatever emotion he may have been feeling hidden by the shadows covering his eyes. Then he pulled her into his arms, his hand cradling the back of her head as he guided it to rest against his shoulder, and held her. Just held her, his arms tight and warm, his embrace somehow comforting.

Courtney cried. She didn't want to, tried to hold it back. She'd cried too many times, wasted too many tears. Tears were worthless, accomplishing nothing except draining her. But she cried anyway, silent tears that burned her eyes and scorched her skin. And Harland just kept holding her, slowly rocking her back and forth, much like she sometimes rocked Noah. She heard him speaking, felt the rumble of the words in his chest, felt the warm air of his breath against her ear. But the words had no meaning, spoken too softly for her to understand.

She had no idea how much time had passed. Minutes? Hours? No, not that long. She sniffled, hiccupped, then pulled back, trying to look away so she could wipe her face. Harland's right arm was still draped around her shoulder, a warm weight that both soothed her and made her wary.

"I got your shirt wet."

Harland laughed, the sound a short choke. "Nah. I'm pretty sure our son did that earlier."

Our son.

Two little words. Simple words. A mere six letters. How could they instill so much fear in her?

And so much hope. Hope? No, that was nothing but foolishness. Nothing but insanity.

She tilted her head, a sense of shyness coming over her

as she watched Harland. He had changed, and not just physically. They had both changed. How could they not have, after everything they had each been through?

But she could still see the boy hiding beneath the hard shell of the man: uncertain of himself, awkward, lonely. Always pushing himself for a sliver of recognition and getting kicked instead. Afraid and pretending not to be, wondering what obstacle life would throw at him next.

Maybe that was why she said what she did. Or maybe she just wanted to give the father of her son a small gift. Or maybe, more likely, she was just simply tired. The reason didn't matter.

Courtney reached out and placed her hand against his cheek. Her fingers trembled against the warm skin, the stubble on his jaw rough yet somehow comforting at the same time. "I don't hate you, Harland. Not anymore. Not for a long time."

His eyes widened, brightened with a flare of...something. She should have seen it coming, should have prepared herself for when he leaned forward, for when his mouth claimed hers.

Prepared herself? No, there was no way she could have prepared for this. His lips were soft, gentle. Coaxing. The kiss so tender, like he was being given a precious gift to treasure. Her mouth opened under his, their tongues meeting in a hesitant reintroduction. Seeking, tasting. Learning again what each had known so well before.

And then Harland pulled away, startling her, leaving her feeling empty. He ran the tip of his thumb across her bottom lip and offered her a small smile.

"I need to go."

She blinked, too dazed to speak. From the kiss? Her reaction to the kiss? Or hearing him say he was leaving? It didn't matter. He leaned forward, pressed another quick kiss against her mouth, then stood up.

"You need to get inside, get some sleep."

Courtney blinked but he was already walking away,

disappearing around the side of the house, disappearing into the shadows.

She pulled the fleece blanket tight around her shoulders, wondering what had just happened.

Wondering how she felt about it. Wondering what she should do about it.

She sat that way for a long time, with no answer except the silence of the night.

CHAPTER FOURTEEN

"So out with it."

"Yeah, man. Details. And a lot of them."

Harland spun the mug of beer between his palms, wishing he could ignore the men on either side of him. Not much of a chance of *that* happening. No, if he wanted to ignore them, he should have never agreed to go with them after the practice. But he did, and now here they were, sitting at the bar inside Mystics.

The place was just starting to fill, mostly with patrons heading to the restaurant side for dinner. The bar area itself was still relatively empty. That would change in a few hours, whenever the night's choice for music—a band or a DJ—showed up. It was a weeknight, so it wouldn't be standing-room-only packed, but it would still be crowded.

And Jason and Zach would probably still be here, looking to hook-up with whoever was on tonight's menu. Was it the place that drew the girls *du jour*? Harland took a sip of beer and looked around, not surprised to see a few of the female patrons already staring, their gazes curious and hungry.

No, it couldn't be the location. He saw the same

reactions, the same come-ons, no matter where they went. It probably had more to do with Zach constantly posting on social media, like he was throwing up a neon sign advertising his whereabouts.

Did Jason do the same thing? Maybe. Or maybe he was just enjoying the side benefits of Zach's constant posting. It didn't matter, not when the end result was the same.

Too bad neither one of them seemed interested in hooking up right now, though. In a few hours, yeah. But right now, Jason and Zach both seemed more interested in pestering the living shit out of him.

Harland took another sip of beer, put the mug down and pushed it away. "There's nothing to tell."

"Oh bullshit. Don't even play that fucking game." Jason's voice was too loud, carrying across the bar. The young girl behind the bar—hell, was she even old enough to be working here?—looked over at them. Even from this distance, Harland could see the faint blush stain her round cheeks.

"Keep your voice down. Christ, Emory. We're not in the locker room."

"Since when do you care?" Jason tried to blow it off but he looked around, seemed to remember where they were, and lowered his voice. "Stop stalling. Now what the fuck did you mean last night when you said you had a kid? Is that why your game went to total shit last year?"

"Yeah, that would explain a lot. It's not like that shit just happens every day, you know?" Zach nudged him with a hard elbow then wiggled his dark brows, like they were sharing some kind of inside joke. Harland rolled his eyes, ignoring the comment about his game. Only he knew the real reason, and it had nothing to do with Noah.

And it wasn't something he planned on sharing with anyone. Ever.

He glanced back at Zach, who was still wiggling his eyebrows like some kind of whack job. "Are you sure you didn't get lead poisoning with your last ink job?"

Zach frowned and glanced down at his arms. The left one sported a full sleeve, a mix of Japanese and traditional, the detail exquisitely done. The start of a partial sleeve covered his right arm from the elbow down. The latest addition—a new school rendering of a hockey player—was still fresh, the skin slightly glossy from the ointment. Why Zach had chosen to get it a few days before scheduled games was a question only he could answer.

He looked back at Harland, still frowning. "Why would you even say something like that?"

"Never mind, it doesn't matter."

Jason leaned in front of him, nearly knocking over the mug of beer Harland had pushed out of the way. "I think he just accused you of being brain damaged."

"I did not." Harland shoved Jason out of the way then started laughing at the outraged expression on Zach's face. "Okay, maybe a little."

"Whatever. Enough trying to change the subject." Zach whistled, the shrill sound splitting the air and startling the girl working the bar. She jumped, nearly dropping the glass she was washing. Zach raised his own glass and pointed toward the three of them. "Can we get three more, sweetheart?"

"Christ, could you be any ruder? And I don't need another one."

"Fine, I'll drink it." Jason downed the rest of his beer then reached for the mug Harland had pushed away. "And he wasn't being rude. That's her job. Lighten up."

"What? To be whistled at like that? Both of you—"

"For fuck's sake, Day-glo, shut the fuck up and tell us what's going on."

Harland leaned back in the chair and blew out a deep breath. He had hoped that maybe he could distract them enough to forget but he should have known better. They edged closer, their expressions turning serious, all joking around forgotten.

"Start talking. What's this about a kid?"

"His name is Noah. He'll be three in April." *Three.* Harland still couldn't believe it. He had missed so much, all because of his own arrogance, his own selfishness. Because he had believed—no, he couldn't blame anyone else. The fault was his and his alone. He'd made mistakes, so many mistakes. But no more.

He had wanted to tell Courtney that last night, had tried but couldn't find the right words. He'd managed to get out *I'm sorry* then fumbled everything else. And then he'd seen the tears in Courtney's eyes, *felt* her despair, and all he could do was pull her into his arms and hold her.

And hope that maybe she could feel just a little of what he felt.

But he hadn't meant to kiss her. Hadn't even considered the possibility. And God, it had been so hard to stop, so hard to pull back when all he'd wanted to do was pick her up and carry her inside and—

"Day-glo!" Jason waved a hand in front of him, making him jerk back. "Christ, man, what is your fucking problem? Stop zoning out."

"How are we just now hearing about this kid of yours?"

Harland turned to Zach then looked away and shrugged, embarrassed. And he suddenly wished he was anywhere but here. He didn't want to be sitting at a bar, talking to his teammates about personal stuff—not when he was still trying to come to terms with all of it himself.

He snagged the mug from Jason's hand and took a long swallow. "I just found out."

"What? No fucking way."

"Yeah."

"So what do you do now?"

"Whoa, back up." Zach leaned toward them, interrupting Jason with a quick slash of his hand. His brows lowered over dark eyes. "You're telling me you just found out about this kid? And you're totally cool with it? Are you even sure it's yours?"

"*He.* Not it. And yeah, I'm sure he's mine."

"How can you be sure? I hope to hell you're not just taking some bunny's word—"

Harland leaned forward so fast that Zach actually jumped back. He didn't hide the anger flashing in his eyes when he spoke. "She's not a bunny so shut the fuck up. Noah's mine. No doubt about it."

"Okay, whatever. Calm the fuck down. I didn't mean anything by it. I just want to make sure your back is covered, that's all. I mean, three fucking years is a long time not to know about a kid, you know?"

Yeah—except he *had* known, because Courtney had told him. He had just refused to believe her, had chosen to believe his old man instead. Yeah, because his old man had always had his best interests at heart, right?

Jason propped his elbow on the edge of the bar and stared at him. "So answer the question. What do you do now?"

"What do you mean, what do I do now? Noah's my son. I'm his father. I just…act like his father, you know?"

"You think it's that simple?"

"Why wouldn't it be?"

"Come on, Day-glo, you can't be that fucking stupid. Or naive. There's a hell of a lot more to it than that. You have to…well, there's things you need to do. And stuff. Right?"

"Well, yeah. I guess." Harland frowned. Jason had a point, which was scary in itself. There *were* things he had to do—he just wasn't sure what. All he'd been focused on was getting himself listed as Noah's father on the birth certificate. That had been important, for reasons he didn't want to examine too closely. He hadn't thought much past that, other than to make sure he got to spend time with Noah.

"There's school. And college—"

"He's not even three yet."

"You still have to plan ahead. And babysitting and making sure he eats the right things and stays out of trouble when he gets older."

Zach nodded. "Plus you have to decide when you're going to start teaching him to play. The earlier you get him on the ice, the better he'll be."

"Guys, I don't think—" Harland clamped his mouth shut. He'd been ready to tell them Noah was deaf, that he probably wouldn't be playing any sports, but he couldn't. He didn't *want* to tell them that—and he didn't understand why. He wasn't ashamed, wasn't embarrassed. At least, he didn't think he was. He had tried to keep his worries, his own questions and doubts about Noah's deafness, to himself. Tried to keep them buried so he didn't have to think about them, didn't have to face the fear that maybe *he* was the cause. Because he couldn't bear that.

And he wasn't ready to share that much about his son anyway. Not that it mattered, because neither Jason nor Zach were paying him any attention.

"Kids his age walk, right?"

"Yeah, of course they do."

Zach seemed relieved by the answer. "Cool. Then you can start getting him on the ice now."

"I don't think—"

"Zach's right. And I know the perfect time: in a few weeks for that family picnic team bonding shit Coach is forcing on us."

"Guys, I don't—"

"That's a perfect idea. That way we can meet the kid, too." Zach downed his beer then slid off the stool, his gaze already focused on the trio of girls at one of the corner tables. "Enough of the adulting. It's time to have some fun. You guys coming?"

"I'm passing."

"Christ. You have a kid and already you're acting like a fucking stick in the mud. You're not married, Day-glo. No responsibilities, no obligations. Right? No need to take yourself out of the game."

Harland refused to answer the silent question in Zach's

intense gaze. How could he, when he didn't know the answer? No, there was no commitment between him and Courtney, hadn't been for a long time.

But he wanted there to be.

The realization slammed into him. Holy fuck. Where the hell had that thought even come from? From nowhere, that's where it had come from. But had it really? Or was it something that had been there, hidden in a secret corner of his heart since he had learned the truth about Noah? Or had it been there before then? Why else would he have kept driving by Courtney's house these last few months?

No. No, it was crazy. Insane. Nothing more than the beer going to his head.

"Man, you really are pathetic." Zach shook his head then walked away, calling out to the giggling group of girls staring at him.

"What did he mean by that?"

Jason shrugged and pulled out his wallet. "Got me. Might have something to do with that stupid fucking look on your face.

"What look?"

"Nothing. Forget it." He slid off his own stool then called over to the girl behind the bar. "Hey, sweetheart. The check?"

Harland frowned and looked away from Jason, trying to figure out what the hell he was talking about. His gaze landed on the girl, saw the way she fumbled with the check, the way she nearly stumbled in her haste to bring it over.

A shy smile teased the corners of her mouth as she pushed the check toward Jason. Long dull brown hair, straight and lifeless, fell into her face, practically hiding all of her features. But it wasn't enough to hide the crimson flush spreading across her cheeks when Jason grabbed the check, his fingers brushing hers.

He glanced down at it, yanked a few bills from the wallet, then tossed everything down on the bar without even looking at the girl. Disappointment filled her face as she collected the money—and just stood there.

Harland thought about hitting Jason, thought about nudging him or saying something to get him to at least *look* at the girl. Or to say thank you or whatever because it was obvious she had a crush on him. He changed his mind. Jason would be oblivious at best. At worst, he'd make a joke of it and end up hurting the girl's feelings, even if he didn't mean to. And she wasn't his type, not even close to being his type. Not just in the looks department—he was pretty certain this girl lacked the biggest thing that attracted Jason: a desire to be nothing more than a fun one-night stand.

Jason shoved the wallet back into his pocket then clapped Harland on the back. "You have fun doing that whole grown-up thing. I've got better things to do."

"Yeah. Whatever." Harland didn't bother watching Jason walk away—he was too busy watching the girl, seeing the way she stared after his teammate. Maybe it was the wistful expression on her flushed face, or maybe it was just his own sudden revelation—and the realization that it was nothing more than a hopeless fantasy. Whatever the reason, he felt a sudden kinship with the girl. Two lost people reaching for something they could never have.

He leaned forward, caught her attention and offered her a gentle smile. "You deserve better, kiddo. He's not worth the heartache."

Harland ignored the shocked expression she turned on him and slid off the stool. The advice he gave her echoed in his ears as he walked out.

Not worth the heartache.

Why had he chosen those words? Why not headache? Or trouble? Or a dozen other different words? Why heartache?

You deserve better. He's not worth the heartache.

A chill went through him as he climbed into the SUV and started the engine. The advice he had just given the poor girl was the exact same advice someone could give to Courtney—for the same exact reasons.

No, for even more reasons. *Better* reasons.

Now it was his job to prove the advice wrong. To prove to Courtney that he was worth it.

That *they* were worth it.

CHAPTER FIFTEEN

Courtney ran a comb through the girl's wet hair then pulled a few strands through her fingers, eyeing the length. She made a few quick snips with her scissors and released the strands, then repeated the process.

The motions were smooth, almost hypnotic. Therapeutic, even.

"So what are you going to do?"

Courtney leaned across the girl—she thought her name was Shannon—and grabbed another pair of scissors from her work tray. "I have no idea."

"Well, I think you should go." Beth met her eyes in the large mirror and winked, then used her scissors to even the length of her own client's hair. "It'll be fun. Lord knows, you deserve to have some fun."

"My idea of fun is *not* being forced to spend time with a bunch of people I don't know. People I don't *want* to know and that I'll never see again."

"Well, you're going. That's all there is to it." Beth paused, shot her another meaningful look in the mirror. "Because Noah needs to go."

Leave it to Beth to get right to the point and throw that

out there. Courtney wanted to disagree with her. Noah didn't *need* to go. In fact, Noah was the main reason she didn't *want* to go. She was afraid it would be too much for him. Too overwhelming, too hectic, just...too much, period.

Harland didn't see it that way.

He didn't see anything wrong with throwing Noah into the midst of a bunch of strangers. Add in the fact that the strangers—and everyone else—would be on skates...on the ice...*skating*...it was a bad idea. Period. Only Courtney seemed to be the only person who thought so. Even her mother thought it was a good idea, a chance for Noah to spend more time with his father. Of course, her mother also thought it was a good idea because that meant Courtney would be spending more time with Harland.

No, she hadn't said as much. At least, not in plain old English. But she knew her mother was hoping that this would somehow get Courtney and Harland back together. Her mother was still convinced—even after everything that happened—that they belonged together. That they were meant to be together.

Nothing was further from the truth. Courtney had no intention of ever getting back with Harland. Of even *thinking* of getting back with him. There was too much history. Too much pain—and absolutely no trust.

So what if he'd kissed her? It was a kiss, nothing more. It wouldn't happen again, even if she couldn't stop thinking about it.

Thinking about *why* it happened.

"Ow." The girl in her chair grimaced and moved her head.

"Oh. Sorry." Courtney gentled her hold on the girl's hair and forced herself to relax—and to stop thinking of Harland and any ulterior motives he might have.

"You're going. No more discussion so you might as well just resign yourself to it."

"Beth, I don't think—"

"Well I think she's right." Shannon's bright eyes caught hers in the mirror. "I think it's so romantic. You just *have* to go."

Courtney paused with the scissors mid-air. "Romantic?"

"Totally. Your long-lost love comes back after being gone for so long and discovers he's the father of your son? And now he's obviously trying to make up for it. Too woo you back and prove his worth." The girl sighed, a dreamy glow in her eyes.

Courtney blinked. Long-lost love? Prove his worth? What fantasy world was the poor girl living in? She wanted to tell the girl there was so much more to it than that. Wanted to tell her it was too late.

Where had Harland been during the long months of pregnancy, when she could barely keep food in her stomach? Later, when she couldn't even bend over to tie her own shoes and then had to be confined to bed because of the complications? Where was he during the agonizing forty-two hours of labor, when she wanted nothing more than to die if that meant making the pain stop?

And later, during the first few months of Noah's life, when he'd been sick? When she knew something wasn't right and the doctors kept brushing off her concerns as nothing more than the hysterics of a young single mother. Or when she learned that he was deaf, that her precious son would never hear the sound of her voice. Running back and forth to doctor after doctor, clinic after clinic, office after office. Hoping. Always hoping…and learning that her hopes were nothing more than wispy dreams, carried off by the harsh wind of reality.

Harland had been there for none of that. And yet this girl could sit there and tell her it was *romantic*? Like taking Noah to a team picnic—and forcing her to go at the same time because there was no way she'd allow Harland to take Noah without her—somehow made up for everything else?

She opened her mouth to say that, to let the girl in on

some harsh life lessons. Beth caught her attention in the mirror, frowned and shook her head. The words died in Courtney's mouth, leaving bitterness in their wake.

The two younger girls continued to talk, spinning wild fantasies of romance and lost love. Of second chances and happy-ever-after. By the time Courtney finished the girl's hair, a headache throbbed at the back of her skull and her jaw ached from clenching it so tightly.

Beth locked the doors and closed up the register, taking a few minutes to make sure the front area of the salon was neat and tidy. She came back and leaned against her work station, folding her arms under her ample chest. "You can relax now, everyone's gone."

"What makes you think I'm not relaxed?"

"Oh, I don't know. Maybe that muscle jumping in your jaw. Or the way you're about to break the broom handle from holding it so tight."

Courtney shot her a dirty look then continued sweeping up the remnants of hair. She scooped everything into the long-handled dustpan then walked to the back room. Beth followed her.

"So what's the real reason you don't want to go?"

Courtney emptied the dustpan then put it and the broom away. She could feel Beth's gaze on her the entire time, knew her friend would just keep staring at her until she finally answered.

"Because I don't understand what Harland's doing. I don't understand what his reasons are."

"Maybe he's just trying to be a dad?" Beth didn't do a very good job of keeping the doubt from her voice.

"I doubt it. I mean, I haven't seen him in three years, and we didn't part on very good terms. Now, all of a sudden, he's back and thinks he can just step in as a dad? It doesn't work that way."

"Maybe that's the only way he knows. I mean, to get involved in Noah's life, you know? I'd have to give him points for trying."

"That's just it, though. Normal people don't just show up and pretend things didn't happen. I mean, he comes by the house almost every evening now and he just acts like—like everything is so damn normal. Like we're just one big happy family and everything that happened in the past doesn't matter."

Beth moved to the small refrigerator and pulled out two bottles of water. She tossed one to Courtney then uncapped the other, her face scrunched in thought. "Maybe that's his way of dealing with it. Maybe he just wants to try for normal. People can only go by what they know. Is that what his parents do? Just act like everything is normal?"

Courtney's hand tightened around the plastic bottle so hard she was surprised the lid didn't shoot off. She took a deep breath and forced herself to relax, forced the memories and the hatred away. "His mother walked out on him when he was five. And his father is a lying, meddling bastard."

"Okay then. So there's some unresolved issues there."

"You think?"

"Are you going to share exactly what happened?"

"Not anytime soon."

"Fair enough. I won't push." Beth took a sip of water then grinned. "Yet. At least, not much."

"Don't even try. I'm serious, Beth. It's not something I'm going to talk about so don't even go there."

Beth watched her for a long minute, studying her, trying to see behind the barriers Courtney had built. She must have realized it wasn't going to work because she uttered a small grunt and nodded. "Okay, I won't push. But maybe that's why he's doing what he's doing. Maybe that's the only way he knows how to try."

"But try *what*? That's what I don't understand."

"Be the kind of father he never had?"

"And what happens when the novelty wears off? What happens when he realizes there's more to being a dad than just stopping in and...and playing games and bringing toys and peeing standing up?"

"Uh...what was that last one?"

"Nothing. It doesn't matter." Courtney pulled out one of the small chairs and fell into it. "What am I supposed to do when he changes his mind? Or when he decides hooking up with some bimbo is more important than spending time with Noah? When he just decides it isn't worth his trouble anymore and he disappears?"

"Is that what happened before?"

"What?"

Beth sat in the chair next to her then leaned forward and placed her hand on Courtney's. "Was he seeing someone else when you guys were together? Is that why you stopped seeing each other?"

"No. No, that wasn't why." Courtney shook her head to emphasize her answer. That much she knew was true. Harland had never even looked at another girl the entire time they were together. But afterwards? Well, if even half the stories she had seen and heard were true, he'd definitely made up for it.

"You never really told me what happened with you guys."

"Yeah, well. I'm not going to start now. It's complicated. And it's in the past."

"You don't sound too sure about that." Beth watched her for a few seconds, no doubt hoping that Courtney would change her mind and share some details. She must have realized that wasn't going to happen because she sighed and sat back in her chair. "I don't know what to tell you, Courtney. I mean, for right now, at least, it looks like he's trying. I don't see how you can stop him from doing that at least."

"I know. I'm afraid if I do, he'll see his attorney and try something else."

"You mean like custody or something?"

"I don't know. He didn't come right out and say it but

he was pretty adamant about making sure he I gave him time to spend with Noah. And since we were at his attorney's office getting the paperwork for the birth certificate straightened out..." Courtney finished the sentence with a tight shrug. She didn't know if it had been a threat on Harland's part or not but she couldn't take the chance that it wasn't, not when she couldn't afford to fight him on it.

"I wish I knew what to tell you, Courtney. Maybe he really is trying, maybe you're worrying over nothing."

"And what happens if it turns out I'm right and he ends up hurting Noah? What am I supposed to do then?"

They were quiet for a long time, the silence holding the answer that neither one wanted to put into words. There wasn't anything Courtney *could* do, at least not yet. Just wait and see and hope for the best.

Except Courtney had given up on hope years ago, and she didn't think she had the strength to fight for it now.

Beth finally pushed away from the table, a bright smile on her face. "Well, sitting here expecting the worse isn't going to help. Come on, let's lock up and get out of here. I have a hot date in a few hours."

"Who with this time?"

"Adam."

"I thought you guys broke up?"

"We weren't together to 'break up', we just weren't seeing each other."

"So what changed?"

Beth waited by the back door, her hand hovering above the light switches as Courtney shrugged into her coat. "I was in the mood for a booty call. And his hose is irresistible."

"I can't believe you just said that. No, wait. Yes I can." Courtney grabbed her bag and pushed on the door. A blast of frigid air wrapped around them and she shivered. "Does Adam know you're just using him for his body?"

"Hey! How do you know he's not just using me?"

"Really? With all the comments you constantly make about his hose and booty calls?"

"I'm a liberated woman, what can I say?"

But Courtney didn't miss the brief shadow that crossed her friend's eyes, or the forced cheer in her voice.

And she realized that maybe she wasn't the only one afraid to face the truth, afraid to admit to emotions better left ignored.

Or the only one afraid of being hurt again.

CHAPTER SIXTEEN

Harland glanced at the board book to his left then over at the computer screen. His tapped the mouse over the painfully short and quick video, watched it play, paused it and hit replay.

Glanced at the picture book once more then back at the screen, studying the finger positions of the oversized hand in the illustrations above the video before copying them.

Dog.

Okay, he was pretty sure he had that one right. He hoped.

He flipped the cardboard pages of the book back to the beginning and started over.

Cat. Dog. Fish. Rabbit.

He made the signs for each, stopped to make sure he was doing them right, then went through it one more time. The book was similar to one he'd seen Courtney read to Noah. She'd flip through the pages, point to an animal, and would Noah make the sign. A huge grin would spread across his face and his eyes would light up with each answer. Then he'd pick out a picture and wait for Courtney to make the sign, almost like he was testing her.

And then Noah had brought the book over to Harland and climbed on his lap. He opened it up with great care and pointed to a picture of a big brown horse, then looked at Harland. Waiting. Expecting him to play the game, to make the correct sign.

Harland shook his head, shot a look of desperation in Courtney's direction. He didn't miss the disappointment on his son's face, like he had somehow let him down by not being able to play the game.

Harland had stopped by a chain store on the way home that night and purchased several children's board books: animals, objects, shapes, colors. He loaded his arms with them, one after the other. And when he got home, he'd ordered a basic book on sign language and started searching for ASL sites on the internet.

He didn't want to disappoint Noah again, couldn't bear to see that expression on his son's face again. So he locked himself up in the spare bedroom that passed for an office for an hour before he crashed each night and studied the most basic of signs.

He extended the index and middle fingers of his right hand, holding them tight together. The letter 'H'. Then he raised his hand, placed his thumb against his temple, and bent and unbent the two fingers making the 'H' twice. *Horse.*

"Yeah. Take that, you stupid fucking horse." Okay, maybe it wasn't the most grown-up thing to say. He didn't care, there was nobody here to see him, not back here. And it meant he could talk to Noah in his own language, at least a little bit.

He closed the picture book and grabbed another one, this one filled with vehicles. He went through each picture, looked for the word on the website he was using. Study the video, learn the sign. Repeat it until he was somewhat comfortable with it and hope he'd remember it when the time came.

Plane. Or airplane. Did it matter? He scrolled up and clicked on 'airplane', watched the oversized hand make the sign. Wait, he knew that one! Well, not really *knew*, but he'd seen it before, when Courtney had signed it after the game a few weeks ago.

He played the short video again, his hand replicating the sign. Easy enough. Maybe. His eye caught the additional text under the video and he leaned forward to read it.

And okay, he'd need to be careful if he ever used that sign because it was damn close to the sign for 'I love you'. Palm down. He needed to remember that: keep the palm tilted down for 'plane'.

Yeah, because if he didn't, he'd definitely crash and burn.

The thought wasn't as funny when he repeated it to himself. In fact, it filled him with a strange sorrow and disappointment. Why was he worried about getting the stupid sign for 'plane' wrong, when he doubted he'd ever have need for the other one?

Stupid. He was just being stupid.

He gathered all the picture books and placed them in the desk drawer. Now it was time to learn some other signs, ones he didn't think Noah would know. He wanted to be ready for the family skate tomorrow evening, wanted to be able to teach Noah some new words.

Hockey.
Ice skate.
Pizza.
Ice cream.

Wow, okay. Maybe he wouldn't do that one because it looked suggestive as hell. If he saw Courtney make that sign, he'd think she was offering—

And fuck, he had to stop thinking like that. Had to stop remembering, stop imagining. It wasn't going to happen, no matter how much he wanted it. Yeah, maybe she told him she didn't hate him anymore, but that didn't mean anything. He saw how uncomfortable she was every time he went over to spend time with them. No, not *them*. With Noah.

But spending time with Noah meant spending time with Courtney because she rarely left them alone. He couldn't blame her, not really. After everything that had happened? After he just showed up and forced himself into their lives? And he wasn't complaining precisely because he got to spend time with both of them.

He gave himself a mental shake, forcing all thoughts of Courtney—and ice cream cones—from his mind. Time to focus on building his limited vocabulary.

Play.
Fun.
Friend.
Father.

Harland stared at the screen, his entire body frozen. If he was smart, if he had any survival skills at all, he'd scroll right past that last one and pretend he never saw it.

His hand hovered over the mouse, his finger shaking. He couldn't do that to Courtney. She'd be furious. Hurt. She'd probably kill him.

Don't do it. Don't do it.

Fuck it. He had never been accused of being smart. He took a deep breath and clicked on the short video, hit it again and again. He curled his hand into a fist, thinking, hesitating.

Then he opened his hand, spread his fingers wide and held them up, tapped his thumb against his forehead.

Father. Dad.

He repeated the sign once more, then a third time.

Father. Dad.

He was Noah's father, dammit. Why shouldn't he know the sign? Why shouldn't he teach it to his son?

He scrolled down, highlighted 'mother', watched the quick video. He recognized the sign immediately, had seen Noah make it often. The sign was similar to the one for 'father', except instead of spreading his fingers wide and tapping his thumb against his forehead, he tapped his thumb against his chin.

Against the forehead: *Dad.*

Against the chin: *Mom.*

Great. So now what? He knew the sign. Good for him. What was he supposed to do with it, now that he knew it? Could he really risk pissing off Courtney? No, it was more than that. It would hurt her. Hadn't he hurt her enough already?

But he was Noah's father. Didn't that count for something?

He knew Courtney would say no, it didn't. She didn't need to come out and say it but it was clear she was convinced he didn't plan to stick around. He could see it in her deep brown eyes each time he stopped by, see it in the set of her shoulders and the carefully blank gazes she tossed his way when she didn't think he was looking. And he could feel it in the waves of sorrow and uncertainty that rolled over him whenever he was near her. He hadn't wanted to admit it because admitting it hurt too much.

It was time to stop playing games. She had to realize he wasn't going anywhere. The only way to do that was to show her. To prove it to her. He wasn't an idiot, no matter how much he acted like one at times. It would take one hell of a lot more than using the sign for 'father' to prove anything to her.

But it was a start. Maybe.

Or it could totally backfire and completely blow up in his face and make the situation even worse.

So what the fuck should he do?

He turned the computer off and sat back in the chair, his hands folded behind his head. Minutes went by, filled with nothing but the muted sounds of the television playing in the living room. It was a distraction he didn't need, an intrusion he didn't want.

He sucked in a deep breath and held it until spots

swam before his eyes. Released it and held it again. It was either that or go out into the living room and have it out with his old man again. Experience told him it was better to stay in here, if for no other reason than to save some of his sanity.

For now, at least. Because a half-baked plan was forming in his mind. Nothing concrete, just wisps of maybes and what-ifs. He was almost afraid to let the wisps take form into something more solid. Not because the hazy plan scared him—it did. Actually, it terrified him. But he was more terrified of what might happen if he didn't at least try.

He'd given up once and walked away without a fight— unless you counted the one he caused because it was easier that way. Harland didn't want easy anymore. He wanted a life—*his* life. The life he should have had but kept throwing away every chance he got—with both hands.

He was tired of his half-ass existence, tired of settling because he was afraid to take chances. Afraid of trying and failing. He thought he'd been playing the game but he hadn't been, not really. He'd been playing it safe, instead.

Well, no more. It had to be all or nothing from this point out. And if he failed, then he failed for real.

And that terrified him most of all.

CHAPTER SEVENTEEN

"Christ, Courtney. It's an ice rink, not Antarctica. He doesn't need all that crap."

Courtney fought with a struggling Noah, finally getting the knit cap over his head. He made a face that let her know exactly how unhappy he was with it and reached up to pull it off.

"No." She brushed his hands away and tied the strings under his chin, ignoring the man standing next to her. What did he know, anyway? No, it wasn't the Antarctica, but it was still chilly in here. Harland might be used to the cold but Noah wasn't. And neither was she.

Her gaze slid to the side, watching Harland as he stood there. He was dressed in jeans and an old sweatshirt, looking entirely too comfortable and completely relaxed and at home. Well, except for the expression of impatience on his face. It was an identical match to the one on Noah's. God, could they look any more alike? Same color hair, same color eyes, same stubborn mouth. Noah's face was more rounded now, with full cheeks flushed with excitement. Would his face become leaner in a few years? Would his jaw become a little more defined, more sculpted like his father's? Probably.

Harland noticed her watching him and raised his brows. "What?"

"Nothing." She turned back to Noah then looked down at the mittens in her hands. Should she make them wear them? They were the kind where the top section folded back to expose the fingers. She had tried gloves but he hated them, probably because the material was too bulky around his small fingers. The mittens were the only kind he would wear—when he didn't bother to take them off and throw them somewhere. But at least she could get them on his hands without too much of a fight, something she'd never been able to do with regular gloves.

Usually.

She looked over her shoulder at the people already skating on the ice. Small groups of twos and threes, mostly adults. There were a few kids there, some around the same age as Noah. None of them had on gloves.

Well, she didn't care what the other kids had on. She gritted her teeth and prepared for battle.

"Courtney, really?"

"You're not helping." She caught one of Noah's hands and gave him a stern look as she tried to get the mitten on. He yanked his hand away and shook his head, grunting in distaste.

"Noah Robert, I swear, if you don't stop fighting me—"

"Here, let me." Harland reached for the mitten and nudged her out of the way. She felt a brief moment of satisfaction when Noah struggled just as much for Harland as he had for her—until Harland leaned forward and gave him a stern look.

He formed his fingers into the proper shape and made one quick sign. "No."

Noah stopped squirming. He didn't look happy about it at all, not with the way his face was scrunched up. But he didn't put up a fight the way he had with her and Harland was able to get both mittens on. He folded back the tops and clipped them in place with the little snap, then lifted Noah from the bench and placed him on his feet.

It wasn't right. In fact, it was totally unfair. Harland was the one he should have been struggling with, not her. But the exact opposite was true. And it wasn't the first time, either. In fact, she was starting to notice it more and more.

She'd try to get Noah to do something and he'd put up a small fight. Nothing catastrophic, nothing cringe-worthy, probably nothing more than the terrible-twos finally hitting. Just small little signs of rebellion here and there, like refusing to sit on his potty chair and insisting to stand instead. Or refusing to eat a certain food that he used to like. But as soon as Harland corrected him, the fighting stopped. It was like Harland was now the authority figure instead of her, like Noah was looking more and more to Harland for things.

It made no sense. Harland wasn't around that much, maybe for a few hours, several evenings a week. And he wasn't around on the weekends because he had games. So why the change in Noah's behavior? Harland had only been coming around for a little more than a month. That certainly wasn't long enough for Noah to form some kind of bond with him.

Was it?

She couldn't bear to think that was the case. Couldn't handle the idea of her son getting close to anyone but her and his grandmother. So what if Harland was his father? Noah didn't know that, had no way of understanding it. She wouldn't even know how to explain such an abstract concept to Noah even if she had wanted to.

And she didn't. She didn't even want to think of it, not when she was certain the novelty would wear off and Harland would lose interest. Because he would, she was certain of it.

Wouldn't he?

If she was an outsider looking at the two of them now,

she'd say no. Harland was kneeling on one knee in front of Noah, saying something she couldn't hear from this distance. She could at least admit she was grateful for that, for the way Harland talked to him like he was any other normal kid. A hearing kid. She had been afraid he would act like Noah was dumb, unable to communicate, incapable of thought.

She'd seen it happen before with other people. As soon as they realized Noah was deaf, they suddenly acted like his brain was defective. The first few times it had happened, she'd tried to explain that Noah's inability to hear didn't make him stupid or incapable of understanding. When it continued to happen, she had to force herself not to lash out, to rail and scream. Now she just mostly ignored it. That didn't mean it hurt any less.

But Harland hadn't done any of that. He talked to Noah like he would any other child, treated him like he would any other child.

Treated him like his son.

Even now, bent over as he was, acting like everything was normal. Like he'd been taking Noah on outings since the day he was born. Harland laughed and said something to Noah, then moved his fingers in a few hesitant signs.

Courtney's mouth dropped open. Harland was signing. She frowned, watching as he made the same signs again. What was he saying? She didn't understand—

She snapped her mouth closed and hurried over to the them, her hand closing over Harland's shoulder. "What are you teaching him?"

Harland mussed Noah's hair then stood, facing her with a look she couldn't quite understand.

"Relax. I'm not teaching him how to cuss."

"I didn't think—"

"Really? Judging from the expression on your face, that's exactly what you were thinking." He watched her for a few seconds then wrapped his hand around her arm, slid it down to her hand, and gave her a gentle squeeze. He didn't release her hand when he spoke again. "I was just telling him that I was going to take him out sledding on the ice, that's all."

"You told him—but how? I don't understand."

"I've been trying to learn a few signs. You know, so I don't look like an idiot the next time he brings one of his books over to me." He released her hand and grinned, then started making a few signs. *Dog. Cat. Car. Plane.* Although he messed that last one up, he needed to tilt his palm down a little more—not that she was going to correct him, not when she'd have to explain why. He made a few more signs, a few she didn't know.

"What was that one?"

"Which one?"

"The last one. Like this." She moved her hands, trying to remember the sign he had made.

"That's 'skate'. I think. And this one is 'hockey'." He held his left hand out palm up and curled the index finger of his right hand over it, knuckle down, pulling it back like a scoop. Then he bent down and made the sign again. "Right little man? That's what Daddy does. Play hockey."

Noah laughed and grabbed Harland's hands, silently asking him to do it again. Courtney's heart leapt into her throat and not just at the sight of Harland teaching her son the sign for 'hockey'. No, it was because of what Harland had said.

That's what Daddy does.

The words had come out so easily, so casually. So naturally, like he'd been saying them for all of Noah's life.

She blinked back the tears that threatened to fill her eyes, swallowed back the emotion clogging her throat. She was reading too much into it, attaching too much importance to the words. It was just part of the novelty, that was all.

Harland reached for the small sled resting against the bench and grabbed Noah's hand. Then both of them turned toward her, identical expressions of silent question on their faces. "We're waiting on you."

"What?"

Harland motioned behind her. "You don't even have your skates on yet."

She was saved from answering—from making up an excuse—when two of Harland's teammates came up to them. They were both tall and well-built, close in age to Harland—like almost every other man she had seen here tonight. They looked at her, both offering politely curious smiles, then turned to Harland.

"Well?"

"Well what?"

"You really didn't think you could avoid us all night, did you?" The one with astonishingly ice blue eyes bent down and smiled at Noah. "Hey kiddo. What's your name?"

Courtney stepped forward, ready to grab Noah's hand before he could hide behind her legs. But Noah didn't move toward her, didn't even seem to realize she was standing there. His hand tightened briefly around Harland's and he looked up at his father, as if waiting for him to make introductions.

Courtney stopped where she was, not sure what to feel. Confusion. Bewilderment. And maybe even a little hurt. It was like she wasn't even here, like she had been replaced. Did Harland notice? God, she hoped not. But he bent down to pick up Noah then reached for her, his hand closing around hers and pulling her to his side.

"Guys, this is my son, Noah. And this is Courtney." There had been just the slightest hesitation in his voice before he introduced her. Could she blame him? No, she couldn't. "Courtney, this is Jason Emory and Zach Mummert. They're my teammates."

Jason—the one with the startling blue eyes—shook her hand first. Zach did the same, his hand holding hers for a brief second longer than necessary. She didn't get any odd vibes from him though, despite the collection of tattoos on his arms and the deep brooding dark gaze. No, she got the impression that he was trying to read her, trying to read the situation and figure out exactly who she was to Harland.

Part of her wanted to ask him to tell her if he ever figured it out.

"Hi Noah." Jason leaned closer to Noah and held his hand out. Noah snuggled closer to Harland and stared at the other man's hand. Harland shifted so Noah could see him better.

"Noah, these are my friends—" Harland raised his free hand then stopped abruptly. He looked down at Courtney, a helpless expression on his face. "That's two hands, isn't it? Does he know 'friend'?"

"Yes, he knows that one." Courtney tried to hide her surprise that Harland knew, and quickly made the sign for Noah. The she pointed to each man and made a 'J' and a 'Z'. They were still working on things like names, and she wasn't even sure if Noah would remember, but it was the only thing she knew to do.

Both men just stood there, watching, their confusion evident. Their eyes moved from Courtney to Noah to Harland, then back to Noah. Courtney held her breath, waiting, knowing she wouldn't be able to hold herself back if either of them dared to say something wrong, if they dared to make fun of her son. She wasn't the only one watching them, the only one on the defensive.

"Noah's deaf, guys. He doesn't have two heads. You can stop staring."

Both men immediately looked away, red staining their cheeks. She waited for the stuttered excuses, the mumbled comments, the quick exit. None of that happened. Zach looked back at her, dark brows lowered over intense eyes.

"What did you do for me?"

"I'm sorry?"

"That thing you made for me. That sign. What was it?"

"Oh. Uh, it was just the letter 'Z'."

"Can you show me?"

The request caught her so off-guard that she nearly stumbled back in surprise. She glanced at Harland but he just stood there with a grin on his face, holding Noah in his arms like it was the most natural thing in the world.

She regained her balance—no, it was more like her *world* regained its balance, a balance she didn't even realize had been missing. It made no sense but for once, she didn't look into it too deeply. Not when these big athletes, men who were so tough out on the ice, seemed to be so accepting of her son.

She showed each of them how to make the letter signs. Then they wanted to know how to sign Noah's name. Before she realized what was happening, a few more of Harland's teammates had wandered over, taking turns to hold Noah as they each learned a few simple signs.

Courtney kept hold of her composure the entire time. At least, she tried. Harland looked over at her a few times, concern in his eyes, silently asking if she was okay. Was she? Yes, she realized. She was. She shouldn't be, though.

She hadn't wanted to come tonight. Not just because she was dreading the forced time with Harland, although that was a big part of it. She had been dreading the reactions to Noah, the whispers and the condemning looks, the condescending attitudes of misunderstanding.

Never before had she been so wrong. And she realized she was guilty of the exact same thing she had been afraid of: superficial judgment. She hadn't even thought to consider that these men, these tough, hard-hitting, no-nonsense athletes, would welcome Noah as if he was part of their family.

Maybe because he *was* part of their family. He was Harland's son, automatically accepted.

And that part *did* scare her. Not that they were automatically accepting of Noah, but that she had been so wrong. Because if she had been wrong about that, what else was she wrong about?

She looked over at Harland, at the way he held Noah. At the way Noah held onto him, so relaxed and trusting. Father and son. Was she wrong about Harland? Was she judging him on an assumption? On emotion based in the past? No, she wasn't foolish enough to think she was falling in love with him again. Wasn't foolish enough to think anything would ever change between them. But he was Noah's father. Maybe this wasn't just a novelty for him. Maybe he didn't plan on disappearing when things became inconvenient.

God help her if that was true, because she had lied to herself earlier. No, she wasn't foolish enough to fall in love with him again…

She had never stopped.

CHAPTER EIGHTEEN

"Is everything okay?" Harland's voice was a little too loud, shattering the silence of the dim living room. Courtney flinched then glanced over her shoulder at him. Her delicate brows lowered over shadowed eyes and he wished he could see them better, see what she was thinking, feeling. But she was standing over by the entertainment center, her back to him.

And she was quiet. Too quiet. She'd been like that most of the night but he had chalked it up to being in a strange place around a bunch of people she didn't know. But she'd been quiet even after they got back here, while they gave Noah his bath, even while Harland read Noah his bedtime story, such as it was.

She didn't even say anything an hour ago when her mother announced she was going to bed, reassuring them that she was so tired she'd even sleep through a jet crashing next door. Harland had choked back a stunned laugh at the pronouncement but Courtney had looked absolutely mortified.

She didn't answer him so he moved closer to her. Stopped, hesitated. Should he just leave instead? Probably.

But he didn't want to, not with her like this, so quiet and faraway.

He closed the distance until he was standing just behind her, mere inches separating them. He could feel the heat of her body, smell the faint scent of her perfume. And he could feel her tension, her confusion and sadness. He raised his hand, held it above her shoulder for a second and told himself that he was only imagining the trembling of his fingers. Then he lowered it, gently closing it over her shoulder.

"What's wrong?"

She shook her head but didn't turn around. And she didn't shrug his hand off, either. Was that a good sign? He stepped to the side and peered into her face, saw her gaze focused on the collection of framed pictures huddled on the entertainment center. One in the back caught his eye, made his breath hitch in his chest as memories assaulted him.

It had been taken maybe seven years ago. Courtney would have been fourteen, which meant he'd been sixteen. The picture had been snapped while they'd been playing Frisbee out back. He'd been holding the cheap plastic disc up in the air, keeping it away from Courtney, teasing her. She was just getting ready to lunge for the Frisbee when her mother called their names. They had both turned and Courtney stumbled and fell into him.

The picture captured them seconds before they fell. Both of them were looking at the camera, surprised smiles on their sun-kissed faces. One of Harland's arms was wrapped around Courtney's waist, the other still held high, holding the Frisbee away from her.

They'd been friends for years before then, neighborhood kids who had somehow found what they were missing in each other. And they'd been nothing more than close friends when the picture was taken. But even then Harland knew there was something different about the friendship, had sensed there was something much deeper between them. Had Courtney known? Had her mother?

He reached out and ran a finger around the picture frame, a ghost of a smile on his face. The smile faded when he noticed the other pictures, saw that he was in a few of them. He pulled his hand away, curling it into a loose fist as he cleared his throat.

"I'm surprised you still have these. I figured you would have gotten rid of them."

A sad smile flashed across Courtney's face, there and gone. She picked up the one of them with the Frisbee and shook her head. "No. I wanted to. I wanted to burn them. But Mom wouldn't let me. She said it would be like destroying a large piece of my life and that I'd regret it if I did."

She stared at the picture for a long moment then carefully put it back in its place. "She was right. As usual."

Harland didn't miss the sadness in her voice, the wistfulness beneath the words. He didn't stop to think, just wrapped his arms around her and pulled her to him. Her body tensed and he silently cursed himself, thinking this was just one more mistake in a long line of mistakes that he'd made throughout his life.

But then Courtney sighed, her warm breath tickling the sensitive skin of his neck. Her body relaxed against his as her arms slipped around his waist. His heart slammed into his chest, its steady beat loud and hard. Did she feel it? Did she know how good it felt just to hold her? How much being able to hold her meant to him? It was like she had thrown him a lifeline, one he hadn't known he needed.

But it had always been that way with her. Even when they were younger, when they were nothing more than friends. She'd always been his lifeline, his hope, his salvation. Did she know that? Had he ever told her that?

Would she even believe him if he told her now, after everything that had happened between them? After everything he had done to her?

He pulled back, needing to tell her, whether she believed him or not. She tilted her head and looked up at him, her pupils dilated, her eyes filled with something he'd seen there before, too many years ago. The words he had wanted to say died in his throat and ended with a kiss.

Their lips touched, hesitant and uncertain. He waited for her to pull back, to hit him, to tell him to leave—but she did none of those things. Instead, her arms came around his neck and her body pressed even closer.

The kiss deepened, mouths opening. Hot, greedy. Their tongues met, seeking, coupling. A harsh groan echoed around them: his, full of desire, despair, desperation. His arms tightened around her, his hands dropping to the swell of her ass. Feeling, touching, relearning the body he once knew better than his own.

He deepened the kiss, drinking from the salvation she offered, then lifted her. She didn't pull away, didn't push against him, didn't hesitate to wrap her legs around his waist. He walked backward until his legs hit the edge of the sofa and dropped into it, Courtney straddling him.

His body was on fire, flames licking his skin with each thrust of Courtney's tongue against his own. With each desperate caress of her hands against his body. His hardened cock pushed against the painful restriction of metal and denim, reaching for the heat of Courtney's body as she pressed her hips into his.

His mind warred with his body, some faint voice telling him to slow down, telling him not to push, not to give in. But his body didn't want to listen, not with the temptation that was Courtney so close.

She'd always been his temptation. His salvation. His life. Always.

Her hands reached for the hem of his shirt, her nails scraping against the heated flesh of his stomach as she raised the shirt. Up, up higher, until he yanked his arms from the sleeves. But he didn't break the kiss, didn't make any move to pull the shirt off. He couldn't bear the thought of losing this contact with Courtney, not even for a second.

She moaned, a breathy sigh that he gladly swallowed. Her hands roamed across his bare skin, her fingers scorching his flesh as she relearned his body. She tangled her fingers in the light spattering of hair in the middle of his chest, flattened her palms against the tight peaks of his nipples. Her hips rocked against him, searching. He cupped her ass in his hands, squeezing. Held her still as he lifted his own hips, pressing the hard length of his cock against her in silent answer.

And fuck, he didn't remember it being like this. Had there always been this sense of desperation? This sense of urgent need, as if his whole existence depended on her? He didn't know, didn't care. All he knew was that he needed her. Now. Needed to become part of her.

Because without her, he was nothing.

He reached for the hem of her sweater, breaking the kiss so he could pull it over her head. Followed it with his own shirt, tossing them both somewhere on the floor behind her. She leaned forward, her eyes closed, her mouth seeking his. Harland shook his head, placed a hand on her shoulder and gently held her in place.

"No. I want to look at you. I need to see you." The voice didn't sound like his, rough and harsh and full of need. Courtney's eyes fluttered open and she tried to shake her head, tried to cross her arms in front of her.

He wrapped his hands around her wrists and tugged on her arms, waited for her to look at him. "Please."

She pulled her bottom lip between her teeth, the action sending a surge of blistering heat through him. Then she nodded, slowly moved her arms to her sides.

Harland lowered his gaze to her chest, sucked in a breath at the sight of creamy flesh held in place by a simple black bra. He raised his hand, traced the edges of the bra with one shaking finger. Her chest heaved under his touch, her breath escaping in a shallow gasp.

He reached behind her with one hand, unsnapped the bra and dragged the material down. Her breasts were fuller than he remembered, still soft yet firm. Her nipples hardened even more under his gaze, tight peaks of temptation. They were darker now, more of a dusky brown than the dark peach he remembered.

He cupped both breasts in his hands, feeling their weight fill his palms. Then he squeezed, ran his thumbs over the hard flesh of her nipples, pinching. She gasped, sucked in a quick breath.

"Did I hurt—"

"No." She opened her eyes and looked down at him, shook her head. "No. They...they're just more sensitive now."

Now. Meaning after having Noah.

Had she nursed his son? Had she held Noah to her breast, given him strength and sustenance from her own body? A wave of possession rolled over him. Powerful. Primal.

He lowered his head, caught one tightened peak in his mouth. Sucked, licked, tasted. Courtney groaned, just a breath of sound, and threaded her hands into his hair, holding him at her breast.

Harland grabbed her hip with one hand, held her still as he drove his own hips toward hers. Over and over as he lavished kisses on her breasts, as he pulled and nipped and sucked.

And fuck, it was too much. Too fast. He wanted to spend hours exploring her body, days relearning each dip and curve. But his need was too strong, desperation driving him.

He reached between them, his fingers fumbling with the snap of her jeans, each motion jerky and awkward. Like this was his first time, like he'd never done this before. Courtney grabbed his wrist, pushed his hand away to take over.

Harland leaned back against the sofa, glazed eyes

watching as she pushed the jeans past her hips. She shifted, moving away from him to slide them down her legs and kick them away.

Harland undid his own jeans, tilting his hips and yanking them down to his thighs. His cock sprung free and he groaned, moved to push the jeans off his legs. But Courtney was in his lap again, straddling him. Heated flesh against heated flesh. Soft against hard.

He dipped his hand between them, ran a finger along her damp folds, stroked the tight bud of her clit. She arched her back, dug her fingers into his bare shoulders. He stroked her again, watching as her hips rose and fell with each touch.

He needed her. Need? No, this was much more than need. Craved, wanted, desired. There was no word that matched what he felt, no word that even came close to describing the knot of emotions possessing him.

He grabbed her hips, settled her pliant body over his—

And stopped. The breath was ripped from his lungs, the sound harsh and desperate. He looked up at her, saw her watching him, confusion mixing with the passion that glazed her eyes.

"I don't have any condoms."

She shook her head, shifted against his hold. "I don't care."

The words hung between them, heavy in the silence. No, not heavy. Freeing. Harland groaned and grabbed her hips once more, bit down on his tongue to keep from shouting when she lowered herself on him. Inch by agonizing inch, his cock entered her wet heat. And fuck, she was tight. So tight. Almost as tight as—

He drove into her, hearing the small gasps of pain mixed with pleasure when he buried himself deep inside. He held himself still, tried to catch his breath when he looked at her.

"Courtney, I—did I hurt you?"
"No."

And God, all he wanted to do was drive into her. Over and over until he lost himself. But he couldn't, not when her brows were lowered over her closed eyes, not when she was biting down on her lower lip, her inner muscles clenching him.

"I couldn't stand hurting you again." His voice was barely a whisper, filled with the sorrow and regret of wasted years. Her eyes fluttered open. She cupped his cheek with one hand and smiled.

"I just need to—it's been…I haven't…"

He heard the words, both what she said and what she didn't say. His heart exploded in his chest, his body igniting with possession. She was his. Nobody else's, even after all this time.

His. Now. Always.

He leaned forward and captured her mouth with his, the kiss deep and needy. Possessing, claiming. His hands tightened around her hips, guiding her as she rode him. Gently at first, then faster. She grabbed his hands, moved them to her breasts, her fingers digging into his wrists as she found her own rhythm.

Driving. Desperate. Powerful. Using him. Making his body hers until her breath escaped on a silent scream and her head fell back, riding him through her climax. He gripped her hips, his fingers rough against her skin, and drove into her. Hard. Fast.

Over and over. Deeper. Frantic. Harder, until his own climax exploded, filling her.

He wrapped his arms around her and pulled her to him, felt her body collapse against his own as he fought for each breath. And then he just held her, their breathing settling, their hearts slowing.

She pulled away first, pressed a quick kiss against his mouth and hurried to the small bathroom. Harland ran a hand through his hair, made an effort to regain his senses as she finished cleaning up before he used the room.

He splashed water on his face then stared at his

reflection in the mirror. Shouldn't he look different? Shouldn't such an earth shattering experience show on his face? In his eyes?

He muttered several colorful words then went back to the living room, took a seat next to Courtney. He was surprised when she slid over next to him, ducked under his arm and rested her head on his shoulder.

"Christ, I feel like I did when we were teenagers, sneaking around all the time." He dropped a kiss on the top of her head, ran a hand along her shoulder. "You don't think your mom knows, does she?"

"She knows. She knew back then, too."

Harland tensed, part of him waiting for something to come flying at his head. Courtney laughed, the sound nothing more than a soft whisper. He grunted in response then reached behind him the for crocheted afghan and pulled it over them.

How many times had they sat like this over the years? On this same sofa, under this same afghan? Watching television, talking, doing homework. Making out. Just being together.

Harland tightened his arm around her, pulling her closer. "Are you okay? I mean with, you know—"

She tilted her head back and placed a finger against his lips, silencing him. "Yes."

Just one single word. Such a simple word—but one with life-altering consequences. Did Courtney know? Did she realize how things would change now? He doubted it. She wouldn't be curled up against him, so calm and relaxed, if she truly knew.

She was his. She had always been his. And he wasn't going to let her go again.

She stirred against him then pushed up, resting her elbow against his shoulder. Harland smiled at the similar pose, remembered how she always used to do that whenever they talked. Correction: whenever *she* wanted to talk.

"So what happened last year?"

"With what?"

She hesitated, her eyes darting away from his for a quick second then shooting back. "With the Banners. With you getting sent back here. What happened?"

"I was an asshole."

"Harland—"

"It's the truth. You keep screwing up, acting like I did, they tend to lose patience."

"But why? What happened?"

He looked away, tried to tamp down the flare of impatience—of humiliation. "Nothing. I don't want to talk about it."

"Harland—"

"I don't want to talk about it, okay? It's not important." No, it was childish. And foolish. And threatened to reopen wounds he thought long-ago healed. But he didn't miss the disappointment in Courtney's eyes when she looked at him. And he couldn't help but feeling as if he had just let her down. That he had just failed at…something.

But she didn't push. And she stopped looking at him, too. Because he'd disappointed her? Or because she simply wanted to rest her head against his shoulder once more?

"Do you think you'll go back?"

"Where? To the Banners? Maybe." Yeah, when hell froze over. He'd done more than just burn those bridges—he'd completely annihilated them. If he was playing at the top of his game, he *might* have a small chance of getting back. Might. But he wasn't playing at the top of his game and hadn't been for a long time.

He waited for Courtney to say something else, to ask him another question, but she stayed silent. He glanced down, saw the shadow of lashes resting against her cheek, saw the gentle rise and fall of her chest.

She was sound asleep. In his arms.

He smiled and pressed a gentle kiss against her temple then settled the afghan more comfortably around them.

He would have preferred having her body curled around his in a bed but this was just as nice.

Courtney was in his arms. It didn't matter where they were, as long as she was with him, where she belonged.

CHAPTER NINETEEN

"What time did Harland sneak out this morning?"

Courtney paused with the coffee cup halfway to her mouth. Her fingers tightened around the handle and she carefully lowered it to the table. Her eyes darted to her mom, expecting to see her standing there, one hand on her hip, a knowing expression on her face. But her mom was standing at the stove, her back to Courtney.

"Uh—"

"I don't know why he didn't just stay for breakfast. There's enough food for him. And I'm sure Noah would have loved for him to stay."

Courtney dropped her head, trying to focus on the paperwork spread in front of her. Heat flamed her face, burning hot enough she was surprised the papers didn't scorch. Was her mother expecting an answer? Some kind of reply? Like what? How could Courtney even think of responding when her brain couldn't even function from embarrassment?

Her mom kept talking, the words holding no meaning as Courtney tried to calm herself down. It was a completely different feeling *knowing* her mother knew than it was just *suspecting* her mother knew.

Courtney turned her head, her gaze darting to the living room. She still couldn't believe they'd done it, right there on the sofa. Again.

Done it? Oh God, she was even starting to think like a teenager again. She wasn't a teenager, wasn't a naïve young girl anymore—hadn't been for a long time. Having sex on the living room sofa while her son slept upstairs just struck her as wrong somehow.

But it hadn't been just sex. No, they'd made love. At least, in her own mind, that's what happened. Did Harland feel the same way? Or was it nothing more than just quick journey into the past for old times' sake?

No, she didn't think so. He'd been gentle in spite of the desperation she'd felt in him. Like being together—like being with her—was more important on a deeper level, more important than he could express with words.

She almost snorted. Yeah, or maybe she was just fantasizing as a way to excuse her own desperation. And she *had* been desperate: desperate to feel him, touch him. Desperate for his own touches, desperate for him to claim her. Desperate to show him without words how she felt.

Well, she had shown him *something*, no doubt about that. She just didn't know what that something was yet. And despite his awkwardness this morning, his hesitation, she didn't regret it. She knew he'd been worried about that, worried that she might be angry or filled with remorse. Or both. For someone who prided himself on being aloof and pretending he didn't need anyone, she had no trouble reading what was under the surface—probably because he'd made no attempt to hide it this morning.

Yeah, and maybe because he'd come right out and asker her, too. Kind of hard to miss when it was that obvious. Did he believe her when she said she had no regrets? Maybe. At least, she thought he did.

Or maybe he was able to see beneath her answer to what she *didn't* actually say. No, she had no regrets about what had happened—but she was disappointed that he'd shut down afterward. He'd been hiding something, refusing to open up about whatever had happened last year. She knew it, and he knew that she knew it.

So why wouldn't he tell her? And did it really matter? In the grand scheme of everything else that had happened between them, did that one thing really matter?

Yes, it did. Because he was hiding something. A piece of him, of who he was, something important. And that, for some reason, bothered her.

"Courtney. Did you hear me?"

"Hm?" She turned back, saw her mom standing there with two plates. She muttered an apology then quickly stacked the papers and moved them out of the way, making room for the plates.

She pushed away from the table, gathered the napkins and silverware and Noah's small sippy cup. Then she went to get Noah. He was on the floor near his toy box, the stuffed plane Harland had given him after the game two months ago in one hand. In his other hand was the small plastic hockey stick he'd been given yesterday. He was taking turns flying the plane then swiping at the rug with the stick.

Courtney stood there for a minute, just watching him. Did Noah understand who Harland really was? Or was he just some man who had suddenly started coming around, nothing more than a stranger who had entered their lives? How could she explain to Noah, to make him understand the truth?

And oh God, did she even want to?

Her eyes darted to the pictures on the entertainment center. Noah wasn't even three yet. Would he be able to recognize Harland from pictures that old? Would any child that young be able to make the connection?

Courtney shook her head then moved toward Noah. She was being silly. Foolish. Stupid. And entirely too nostalgic. She picked up her son, her hand automatically reaching for the toys he refused to drop.

"Come on, kiddo. No fighting today. Mommy's not in the mood. You know toys aren't allowed at the table." Or, in his case, the high chair.

He grunted and shook his head, his arm dodging her reach every time she tried to grab the hockey stick. He did the same when she reached for the stuffed plane. Courtney stopped in the doorway, Noah wiggling in her arms, and looked to her mother for help.

They finally got him settled, the toys placed off to the side where he could see them while he ate. Courtney refilled her coffee mug, made a fresh cup for her mother, then sat down to eat.

She took a few bites, barely tasting the eggs and bacon, then placed her fork to the side of her plate and stared at Noah. He was completely oblivious of her scrutiny, totally absorbed in alternately eating his food and smearing it around his mouth.

"What's the matter, sweetheart?"

"Hm?" Courtney looked at her mother, saw the concern in her eyes. She shook her head and forced a smile to her face. "Nothing. Just thinking."

"About Noah? Or about Harland?"

"I don't know. Both, I guess." Courtney reached for her coffee then let her hand drop to the table. "Do you think he knows?"

"Do I think who knows what?"

"Noah. Do you think he knows Harland is his father?"

Her mother folded her hands in front of her and turned in the chair to watch Noah. She was quiet for several long minutes before turning back and facing Courtney. "I think he might know *something*. They've certainly bonded rather quickly, haven't they?"

"Yeah. I guess."

"Hm."

"What's that supposed to mean?"

"Nothing dear. Eat your breakfast before it gets cold."

Courtney picked up her fork, dragged it through the congealed yolks of the eggs, put it back down without taking a bite. "Should I tell him?"

"Tell who what?"

"Mother! I know you're not that dense. Stop playing games. I'm being serious. I need your advice."

Her mother raised a single brow in her direction. Courtney didn't miss the flash of amusement in her eyes. "Advice about what?"

"Should I tell Noah? I mean, would he even understand? How would I even know if he made the connection? And how would I even let him know?"

"Why the change of heart?"

"What?"

"Why the sudden change of heart? I seem to recall you had a very different opinion not very long ago. That you were very adamant about not wanting Harland in the picture."

Courtney sat back in the chair, her shoulders slumping as she stared at the hands folded in her lap. She let out a quick breath and shrugged. "I was."

"Then what changed?"

"I don't know. I just…" Her voice trailed off, her mind spinning as she tried to answer the question. She just…what? Realized she was still in love with him? Yes, but that had nothing to do with this. Maybe, somewhere deep inside the smallest corner of her heart, there existed the tiniest sliver of hope that things might be different between them. That they might end up back together, try to work things out.

Yes, they'd had sex—made love—last night. Yes, she'd fallen asleep in his arms. Yes, she still loved him. But she was a realist, had been for several years. Making love wasn't a magic pill that would make everything better. She knew enough to be able to separate the two, no matter how much she might wish otherwise.

But it wasn't whatever was between them—or not

between them—that was making her change her mind regarding Noah. It was the way Harland was with his son, the way he slid so naturally into the role of father. She had convinced herself this would be nothing more than a passing phase. A novelty that he would tire of.

She didn't think that way anymore, not after seeing them together. Not after yesterday afternoon at the family skate.

Her mom leaned over and ran one hand along Courtney's arm, much like Courtney did with Noah to comfort him. "So why the change of heart?"

"I just...I'm not sure. No, that's not true. I thought...at first I thought he'd just get tired of playing at something and leave, you know? But after watching him with Noah, watching Noah with him—do you know he's trying to learn different signs? All on his own? And he even taught one to Noah yesterday. 'Hockey'."

Courtney's mother laughed, the sound gentle and soothing. "Well of course he did. Makes perfect sense."

"Yeah." Courtney smiled and looked at Noah. He looked so much like Harland. Had she just blocked that out these last two years? Probably. But she couldn't block it out now. "I was so afraid he'd just disappear again, you know? And I was worried about what would happen to Noah if that happened. But now..."

"Now you think differently?"

"Yeah. I do. Mom, if you could have seen them yesterday. Harland was so protective. And he was showing him off, introducing Noah to everyone as his son. Like it was the most natural thing in the world. Like Noah had always been a part of his life."

Courtney hesitated then reached for her coffee and took a quick sip. She held the warm cup between her hands and stared into it. "I know it's crazy because it hasn't been that long. I mean, what? A little over two months? Compared to more than three years? It doesn't make sense. So why do I feel so certain that he's going to stick around? That he deserves to have Noah realize he's his father? Or is it just wishful thinking and I really am crazy?"

Her mother watched her for a long minute, her gaze direct enough that Courtney had to resist a serious urge to squirm. Then she reached out and placed a gentle hand on Courtney's arm once more. "Do you remember the first day you met Harland?"

Courtney swallowed back the tears at the memory and nodded. How could she forget? She had been seven, and it had been the day of her father's funeral. They had come home, the house filled with strangers speaking in quiet whispers, shooting her looks of sympathy that she didn't quite understand. All she knew was something bad had happened, something sad and terrible that made her mother cry. Made *her* cry.

She had run from the house, carrying a ragged doll that had been a present from her father the previous year. She only made it to the bottom step of the porch before she plopped down, not worried about getting her dress dirty, not worried about anything except the painful lump in her chest. She hugged the doll to her, thinking that maybe if she held it close enough, hard enough, that her father would come back from wherever he had gone.

And then she had cried. Hard ragged tears that made it hard for her to breathe and left her hollow and drained. She'd heard footsteps on the sidewalk in front of her, saw a pair of beat-up dirty tennis shoes. She looked up, saw a strange boy standing in front of her, somehow knew he was the one who had just moved into the empty house the next block over.

He watched her for the longest time through eyes a color she had never seen. Then he asked her why she was crying.

Courtney had wiped her face, not caring about dirt or snot or anything, and told him her father had gone away. He nodded and just kept watching her. Then he told her that his mother had gone away too.

And then he sat down next to her and hugged her with his skinny arms, letting her cry all over the front of his dirty shirt.

Courtney took a ragged breath and wiped the tears from her eyes. She hadn't thought about that day since...she couldn't remember when.

Her mother's voice was shaky when she spoke, filled with long-buried emotion. "I came outside, so worried about you, and saw this boy just holding you. He was dirty and sweaty and so...so *gentle* with you. And when he looked up at me with those eyes—" She took a deep breath and pushed away from the table, grabbed some tissues from the box on the small sideboard. She handed one to Courtney, used the other for her own eyes before she sat back down.

"He had such a fierce look in his eyes. Like he was daring me to intrude, daring the world to hurt you. Like he had just appointed himself your protector and God help anyone who tried to get in his way."

Courtney patted her eyes with the tissue then crumpled it in her hand. "You never told me that."

"Well, to be honest, I tried to forget it, convince myself I had imagined it. I think it scared me a little at the time, seeing something so fierce in someone so young." Her mother blew her nose then reached for her coffee. "Harland has been such a huge part of your life, for so long. I think even then I knew you two would end up together."

"Yeah, well. Not quite."

"Maybe. Maybe not. You never told me all the details of exactly what happened between you two and I never pushed. I was able to piece enough together to figure the gist of it, so I won't push now. But I will tell you this much: not many people get a second chance in life. Very few people even get a first chance at the kind of connection you and Harland have. And no matter what happens, you will always have that connection—and I don't mean just because of Noah. So no, I don't think you're crazy. And no, I don't think Harland has plans on disappearing from Noah's life, no matter what happens with the two of you. Harland isn't his father."

"I know, but..." Her voice trailed off and she looked away, trying to control the chaos swirling through her mind—and her heart. As soon as she tamed a thought, a feeling, it slipped from her grasp and whirled away, leaving her even more confused than she was before.

Was she thinking *too* hard? Trying to be too rational? But what else could she do?

"Have you actually talked to Harland about any of this?"

"About what?"

"About your concerns and worries with Noah. With Harland. With all of it."

"Well, no—"

"Courtney Marie Williams. Do not sit there and tell me you haven't even talked to the man about any of this! Don't you think you should at least do that before working yourself up into these worries?"

"I—but—"

"No buts." Her mother pushed away from the table, reached down and tugged her arm. "Go upstairs, clean up. I'll take Noah to daycare and *you* can get yourself over to Harland's to talk to him."

Courtney opened her mouth to argue. She didn't *want* to talk to Harland, not about this. Not when it meant opening up and admitting her deepest fears. But her mother just stood there, a look in her eyes that promised dire consequences if Courtney didn't obey.

So she sighed and left the room, her feet dragging as she went upstairs, her mind whirling as she thought about what she would say to Harland when she got there.

CHAPTER TWENTY

She'd knock one more time. If he didn't answer the door then, she'd leave because he obviously wasn't home. And oh, God, why had she thought this was a good idea? Why had she let her mother bully her into coming over here?

Courtney took a deep breath, let it out slowly, then raised her hand and rapped it against the door. Not too hard, in case Harland was sleeping. But so softly so she wouldn't have to lie when her mother asked.

And her mother *would* ask, that was a given.

She waited, her head tilted to the side because she thought she heard footsteps on the other side of the door. Maybe it was just her imagination, maybe she should just turn around now and—

The door opened. Courtney's breath left in a rush, like someone had punched her in the stomach. She should have never come here, never listened to her mother. She wanted to turn around, to run and never stop. But her feet were frozen in place, her entire body unable to move as she looked into a face she hadn't seen in almost three years.

A face so much like Harland's. So much like Noah's.

No. No, the face was nothing like her son's. Nothing like Harland's. The physical resemblances were there but that was it. The honeyed eyes staring at her now were cold, flat and unforgiving, devoid of life. This face was harder, with angry grooves pulling at the mouth and harsh lines spreading around the eyes. He may have been attractive years ago, might even still be considered attractive by women who preferred hard and unforgiving men. Men with a razor edge and hearts of stone, men who put nothing ahead of themselves.

Courtney swallowed, tried to look unaffected by the man in front of her, the man she had hoped to never see again.

He leaned against the doorframe, the hint of muscle still clear in the arms he folded across his chest. The plaid shirt pulled around his waist, straining against the extra weight he carried. The jeans he wore were stained, dirty, and she caught the faint whiff of stale smoke.

A cold smile spread across the granite face as he stared at her. "Well, well. Didn't expect to see you again. What do you want?"

"I—" Her voice trembled and she almost stepped back. How could he still have this effect on her? How could he still scare her, after all these years? She had never liked him, not since the first day she had met him. He had been harsh and unforgiving even then. Too tough on Harland, too free with insults and the back of his hand.

But she wasn't that young girl anymore. She wasn't the scared teenager about to become a single mother. She was older now, he shouldn't be able to frighten her the way he had.

Not unless she gave him the power to, and she didn't want to do that, not anymore. So she took another deep breath and reached inside herself for a courage she didn't feel. "I was looking for Harland."

"What do you want with him?"

"I just—I wanted to talk to him."

"Why?"

His questioning threw her, almost like she was being interrogated. Her mind whirled, trying to regain its balance. "I just wanted to talk to him. If he's not here, I'll just come back later."

No, she wouldn't. She would stop by the rink after practice, or call him. Or just wait for him to come by the house. But she would *not* come back here, that much was certain.

She turned around, ready to leave, felt something close over her arm. A gasp of surprise escaped her and she looked down, seeing the large hand clasped around her upper arm. She tried to pull away, felt a second of blind fear.

"What the hell are you up to now? I told you he wanted nothing to do with you."

"Let go of me."

"No. Not until you tell me what you're up to."

"N-nothing. I just wanted to talk to him, that was it." She yanked her arm again, hoping he'd let it go. Let *her* go, so she could just turn and run.

"Isn't it bad enough that you went ahead and had your little bastard after telling him you weren't going to? What do you want now? Money? Are you going to try to bleed my son dry? Too damn bad. Now that he fucked up his play, he's not making the big money like he used to."

"No! I don't want anything from Harland. And Noah is *not* a bastard! He's Harland's son. *Your* grandson!"

"That's not what you told my son, now is it? You admitted the kid wasn't his. Just like I told him it wasn't. You were always too wild for him, even growing up. Always demanding his attention, trying to sink your claws into him."

"That's not true." Courtney blinked back the tears, tried to pull her arm free one more time. Why had she come here? If she had known Harland's father was here, she would have never come here.

And the words…no, she shouldn't be surprised by them. Shouldn't be hurt by them. They were the exact same words he had thrown at her the last time she'd seen him, in the parking lot of the grocery store when she was seven months pregnant.

He had stopped her, hatred and disdain in his eyes as he gawked at her rounded belly. Then he'd all but threatened her, told her to never contact Harland, to never let him know that she was having the baby.

She had been so shocked she hadn't said anything, much like she was right now. Her mother had been with her then, had stepped in front of her and gotten right in Mr. Day's face. Courtney had no idea what her mother had said but the man had scurried away, like he couldn't put enough distance between them fast enough.

She wasn't going to let him do this again. Belittle her, humiliate her. She pulled against his hold, trying to twist her arm from his grasp. "Let go of me!"

"Listen you little whore—"

A flash of something whirred in her peripheral vision, fast and furious. The grip on her arm disappeared and she stumbled back, fighting to catch her balance before she fell. Her arms pinwheeled, searching for something to grab, and came up empty. She landed on her bottom with a small "umph", too stunned to move.

Not because she had fallen.

Because Harland had his father pinned against the wall, his hands twisting the shirt collar tight around his throat. Mr. Day's face was an angry mottled red, his eyes flashing hatred as Harland shook him.

"What the *fuck* are you doing? You touched her? You fucking touched her? Who do you think you are?"

"Get off me, you piece of shit, before I—"

"Before you what? I'm not that little kid you used to smack around anymore. I'm bigger now. And I know how to take care of myself. So tell me, what the *fuck* do you think you can do to me?" The words were cold, made more menacing because they were softly spoken instead of screamed. But Courtney heard the pain underneath, felt the anguish Harland was feeling as he pinned his father against the wall.

She scrambled to her feet, hurried over to Harland and wrapped her hands around his wrists. "Harland. Stop, please. Don't do this. Don't let him do this to you."

She felt the trembling in his arms, felt the tension running through him. Had he heard her? Yes, she could see it in the way his jaw briefly relaxed, in the slight relaxing of his hands.

"Please Harland. You're not like him. You've never been like him." Her voice cracked but she didn't care, just kept pleading, trying to get through to him, trying to banish the image of Harland sitting in jail. Because she had no doubt that his father would do that—press charges against his son, revel in the idea of his own son sitting in jail. "Don't do this. Please. For me."

Time slowed, nearly stopped. Courtney's lungs hurt from not drawing breath; her heart beat fast and heavy in her chest. Harland nodded, just a quick move of his head, barely noticeable. Then he released his grip on his father, shoving him to the side as he stepped back. He grabbed Courtney's hand, tugged her so she was standing behind him. Protecting her, shielding her.

"Get out. Pack your shit and get out. If you're still here when I get back, I'll have you arrested. If anything is missing when I get back, I'll have you arrested. Is that clear?"

The color drained from Mr. Day's face, leaving it a pasty white—a stark contrast from the bright red it had been seconds before. His eyes widened, grew even colder. "You aren't serious. After everything I did for you? All the shit I went through for you?"

"Everything you did? What, Dad? What did you do?"

"Taking you to games, to practices. Pushing you. Making sure you were ready. Everything I gave up for you.

And then this...this little..." He glanced back at Harland, swallowed. "Then *she* comes along and tries to destroy it? And this is how you repay me? By taking her and her bastard's side?"

Harland's hand tightened around Courtney's. Seeking strength? Reassurance? She didn't know. He leaned forward, his voice still dangerously low when he spoke to his father.

"Noah is my son. I'm his father. Nothing you do, nothing you say, nothing you think, will ever change that."

"You? A father? What the hell do you know about being a father?"

"Nothing. But I know what *not* to do: everything you did. Now get your shit and get out."

"You can't mean—"

"Oh, I mean it. I've never meant anything more in my life." Harland stepped back, tugged on Courtney's hand. Then he was leading her outside, across the parking to his SUV. He helped her in, started it up, and drove.

And kept driving, not stopping until they reached the Galleria. He pulled in, drove around until he found a remote spot, away from the crowd of cars, and parked.

He didn't say anything, just sat there, his hands gripping the steering wheel so tightly that his knuckles grew white. But even then, despite that, she could see the trembling in his hands, his arms.

His whole body.

She undid the seatbelt and leaned across the console, moving as close as she could to get her arms around him. He held himself stiff, not moving, barely breathing for the longest time. Then the tension slowly left him, draining away, the trembling easing. He released a ragged sigh and shifted in the seat, folding his arms around her and tugging so she was partly sprawled across his lap.

And he just held her, neither one of them saying a word for the longest time.

Courtney pulled away, just enough so she could see his

face. There was a haunted, dazed look in his eyes. He looked shocked, stunned. Like he wasn't quite sure what had happened. She pressed her mouth against his, surprised at the chill of his lips.

"Are you okay?" He nodded, a short jerky motion of his head. She pressed another kiss against his lips, cradled his cheek with her hand. "Are you sure?"

"Yeah." His voice was hoarse, ragged, like he hadn't used it in a while. He cleared his throat and nodded again. "Yeah. I'm fine."

"Harland, I—"

He shook his head, cutting her off, still not quite looking at her. "I've never stood up to him before. Never. I always did everything he said, always believed everything he said. Never fought back. But when I saw him touching you, heard what he was saying...I lost it. I don't know what happened. I just lost it."

He gave himself a little shake, his eyes slowly starting to focus. He turned to her, fear and sorrow so clear in his gaze. His hand reached for her jacket, started tugging at it. "Did he hurt you? I need to see. I need to—"

"Harland, I'm fine." She grabbed his hand, held it tightly in hers, felt his fingers shaking as they twisted with hers. Her arm still stung and she'd probably have a bruise there, but she didn't want Harland to see. She was afraid of what he'd do if he saw, afraid he'd blame himself for some reason. "I'm fine. It's okay. Everything is okay now."

"Is it? Courtney...God, I can't believe—I am so sorry. So fucking sorry. Can you ever forgive me?"

"Forgive you? Harland, you had nothing to do with this. You're not your father. You're nothing like him." And oh God, it was true. So true—and she had always known that. Deep down, she'd always known the truth. How could she have ever been afraid Harland would be like his father? How could she have ever thought to compare him to his father? She knew better.

But Harland was shaking his head, sorrow and regret

still filling his eyes. "I'm not talking about this. Before. Three years ago, when I—"

"Harland, don't. Please. It's in the past now. It doesn't matter."

"It *does* matter. It's always mattered. I let him talk me into believing that you had slept around. That the baby wasn't mine. He just...he kept pounding it into me, day after day after day until that was all I heard. And I let myself believe him because he was my father. Because he seemed so fucking worried, so fucking concerned. And I thought—"

He sucked in a deep breath, ran a hand over his face, dropped his gaze. She could see the flush fill his face, feel the slight tremors still running through him. "For the first time in my life, I thought he was really concerned. That he really cared. He was my father, why would he lie? So I let him convince me. I *let* myself believe it. And that's something I'll never be able to forgive myself for."

"Oh Harland." She wrapped her arms more tightly around him, like she could somehow take on his pain if she only held him tight enough. She dropped her head on his shoulder and squeezed her eyes against the tears. "It's not your fault. There's nothing to forgive."

"Yes, there is. I wasn't there for you. I wasn't there for Noah. And I missed so much. So fucking much. Those are moments, years, I'll never get back."

They were quiet for a long time, just holding each other. And Courtney knew what she had to do, knew she had the answer to all her unasked questions. No, maybe he would never get those moments back, but she could help him see them. And she could make sure he'd have other moments, every moment that stretched ahead of them.

She didn't need to be afraid, didn't need to let her fear rule her. She just had to trust in herself. In what she felt. In what she knew, deep down in her heart.

What she'd always known.

CHAPTER TWENTY-ONE

Sweat dripped down his face as he raced across the ice, down toward the net. Jason passed the puck; he watched, barely daring to breathe, as it skipped across the ice, coming closer. Harland reached out with his stick, stretching—

The puck hit the blade, bounced, almost slid away until he pulled it in closer. He spun around, swept his left arm out, pushing away the defender creeping up on him. Eight feet. Five feet. The net loomed closer. He darted left, changed direction at the last minute, shot around the second d-man. Close, so fucking close...

He pulled the stick back, held his breath, and took the shot.

The puck bounced off the goalie's glove, hit the pipes, and bounced behind the net.

Fuck!

Harland moved in for it, him and Jason both flying. Jason reached it first, took it around the back of the net, shot it toward the goal.

Rebound.

Harland moved in, got his stick on the puck. Left, right,

left again. Shoot.

Another rebound.

How the *fuck* did he miss that?

Jason slid behind him, moved in to finish the job and—

Score!

The red light flashed soundlessly behind the net and the arena erupted with boos. Harland ignored them, moved in with Kyle and Ben to pull Jason into a group hug, patting him on the back. Then they skated over to the bench, settled down as the first line moved into place for the face off.

Harland reached behind him for a towel, dragged it across his face, then grabbed a bottle and shot a long stream into his mouth. His heart was still racing, but not from exertion, not totally.

He should have had that shot. It had been damn near perfect, his timing just right. How the fuck had he missed? Not once but twice. Every single game. He kept waiting, thinking the next one would be the one.

Only it never was.

Now, instead of waiting to score, he was waiting to be benched…permanently. He was on the fourth line and his ice time sucked. Not as bad as it could, but nowhere near where it used to be.

What made it worse was that he was trying. He was *really* trying. He stayed late after practice, ran extra drills on the ice, spent extra time in the weight room. He didn't want to be a fuck up anymore. *This* was what he wanted. This, right here. The ice and the sweat and the cuts and the bruises. The sore muscles and stiff body. The freedom he felt when he moved across the ice, the exhilaration of winning, the feeling of family. Of being accepted, being part of a team, part of something bigger than just himself.

All of it. He wanted it. Craved it. It was the only thing he knew, one of the few things he had dreamed of. He had come so close to losing it, to throwing it away because of a silly, childish disappointment. He was close to losing it now.

And the thought terrified him.

Maybe he'd never make it back to the pros, maybe his future would always be here. He didn't care, as long as he had it. As long as he could play.

But he was in the middle of a potentially career-killing dry spell, with no end in sight. No matter what he did, nothing seemed to work. And now it was catching up to him, screwing with his mind, with his focus, his concentration.

Because yeah, that was just what he needed: something else to screw with his head, after everything else he'd been through. After everything else he'd screwed up in his life.

Jason nudged him, pulling his attention back to the game—which is where it should have been all along. Harland watched the play on the ice, banged his stick against the boards with everyone else when Zach scored seconds before the final buzzer. They piled out on the ice, congratulating their goalie, Tyler Bowie, on another win.

Then it was back to the locker room for a lecture from the coaching staff, to listen to kudos and criticisms. Harland kept his gaze lowered, afraid of being singled out, afraid he'd see what was coming in the coach's eyes. He didn't want that, couldn't face it.

Then it was time to hit the showers and change, grab his bag and climb onto the bus for the long drive home. They had off tomorrow but he'd still hit the rink, still work on his puck handling and shooting. And then he'd stop by Courtney's and spend time with Noah.

He moved toward the back of the bus, tossed his small duffel bag onto the overhead rack then slid into the window seat. Sleep might be possible—if he could get his mind to clear. If the last two weeks were any indication, he already knew that probably wouldn't happen.

It didn't make sense. If you didn't count his shitty game, things were finally looking up. His father had moved out after that fucked-up confrontation, and he'd done without taking as much of Harland's shit as he had expected. Yeah, because he had expected to come home to a completely empty place. It didn't matter, he was gone. An end to a chapter that had been dragging on for too long.

He was spending more and more time with Noah, settling into something that felt like a comfortable routine. And Courtney had given him a bittersweet gift: pictures and videos of Noah from the last two years. Snippets of things he'd missed, a brief glimpse into life's precious moments.

And Courtney...he wasn't sure how to define what was between them. They had become closer in the last few weeks but how close? It wasn't like it had been before. Would it ever be? No. They were older now, different than the young kids they had been. They spent time with Noah, spent time together. Cuddling, making love, just being together. Being a family.

Only it didn't feel quite right, felt like something was missing, like something was off. Almost like they were just playing at being a family, like she was holding something back.

Or maybe he was, without even realizing it. Or maybe his idea of family was so completely fucked-up that he didn't know what a real family was supposed to be like.

"Are you going to be like this the entire ride back? Because if you are, I don't want to sit next to you."

Harland looked up, frowned at Jason and was ready to tell him he could go sit somewhere else. But he was too late because Jason was already dropping into the seat next to him. Zach and Tyler took the seats in front of them, making him bite back a groan. He should move, maybe go sit next to Aaron so he wouldn't have to listen to shit for the next four hours. Tyler wasn't too bad, usually quiet and pretty even-keeled even if he was a little out there. But hell, he was a goalie—they all had those weird quirks.

Maybe if Harland looked out the window, or closed his eyes and pretended to sleep, they'd ignore him. Yeah, right. That hope only lasted for five minutes after the bus pulled out of the lot.

"You're jinxed."

Harland's eyes popped open and he shot a dirty look at Jason. "What?"

"You heard me. You're jinxed. You can't score to save your life."

Harland shook his head, trying to ignore the words, trying to shake off the icy coldness that swept through him at the words. He didn't buy into a lot of the superstitious shit the other guys did. At least, not most of it. But like every other player he had ever known, he had his own rituals, his own little idiosyncrasies. For Jason to even say the word *jinxed* was throwing out bad mojo Harland didn't need to hear.

Zach turned around in the seat, leaned over the back so he could join in the conversation. Great, just what Harland needed. "Yeah, man. Something is definitely going on with you. You're cursed."

"Fucking shit guys. Would you knock it off? I don't need to hear this shit, okay? I'm trying. It's just a dry spell. Not a jinx or a curse, so just knock it off." He shifted in his seat, let his gaze drift to the scenery passing by the window. Yeah, because the blackness of night broken by the occasional light of a street lamp was so much more entertaining.

"You're trying too hard."

Harland looked up, swallowed a groan when he saw Tyler leaning over the seat as well. Great, even the goalie was getting in on it now. Only he actually looked serious, instead of being a smart ass like Jason and Zach.

Tyler watched him with dark steady eyes filled with a laser focus. The look was made even more intense because he was one of those guys who had those long thick lashes that most women longed for. But he wasn't feminine, not even close. Rugged face, a perpetual scruff that darkened his jaw, long black hair that would be the subject of a hundred different hockey-flow memes if he was in the pros.

Yeah, he definitely had the goalie mojo thing down pat. Too damn bad it was all focused on Harland right now.

"What do you mean, I'm trying too hard?"

Tyler shrugged. "Just what I said. I watched you. You tense up right before you shoot. Always. You're trying too hard."

Jason and Zach both looked at him, disbelief clear on their faces. Then they both laughed.

"Bullshit. There's no such thing as trying too hard."

"Yeah man." Zach rolled his eyes and nudged Tyler with his elbow, hard enough that the other man bumped into the window. "He's cursed. Has been since last year. His game's gone to shit."

"Yeah. So all you have to do is tell us why your game went to shit, and the curse will be gone." Jason leaned in closer. He might be smiling but there was a seriousness in those freaky blue eyes that contradicted the teasing.

Harland shook his head, trying to ignore all three of them. He wasn't telling anyone what happened—not even Courtney, and she might be the only person who understood. But even that was a stretch. How could he expect anyone to understand, when he didn't really understand himself? It was foolish. Childish. And so fucking stupid, it didn't even deserve mentioning.

And it had nothing to do with his game. Nothing. Yeah, maybe he'd lost it last year, let what happened get to him in ways it shouldn't have. Let it throw him off and fuck up his attitude and got him sent back here. But it had nothing to do with his game.

And in some weird, twisted way, he was almost happy it happened. If it hadn't, if he hadn't been sent back here, he may have never found out about Noah.

Jason elbowed him in the side. "Come on. Time to

come clean. What happened last year?"

"Let it go."

"You know what they say: confession is good for the soul."

"Fuck off."

"Touchy, touchy." Jason laughed then settled more comfortably into his seat. Harland looked around, wondering again if it was too late to change seats.

"Fine, don't tell us." Zach leaned even further over the seat, a glint in his eyes. "Tell us about your baby mama. You guys together?"

"Why do you care?"

"Because man, if you're not, I wouldn't mind—"

Harland reached up, grabbed Zach's tie, and yanked. "You stay the fuck away from her."

"Whoa. Fine. Whatever." Zach held his hands up, the teasing gone from his eyes. "I was only messing with you. Fuck. I wouldn't make a play for her. None of us would. You know that."

Harland released his grip and sat back in the seat, took a few deep breaths. Yeah, he knew that, should have known Zach was just fucking with him, trying to get a reaction out of him. Well, he did. Probably not the reaction he was expecting but fuck him. Maybe next time he'd think before running his mouth.

Jason either didn't know when to leave things alone, or didn't care, because he shifted in his seat once more and leaned a little closer. "Seriously though, what's the story? You guys together or what?"

Harland took another deep breath and wondered if he should sit on his hands. If he didn't, there was a very real possibility he'd end up beating the shit out of Jason several times in the next few hours.

He opened his mouth, ready to tell Jason exactly that, when he felt a vibration in his front pocket. The sensation startled him, causing him to jump until he realized it was his phone. Who the hell would be calling him this late?

He knew the answer before the question had completely formed in his mind. He dug into his pocket, grabbed the phone and tapped the screen. There was a second of blackness and he thought maybe he'd hit the wrong button, then the screen cleared and Courtney's face was looking back at him.

He glanced around, saw that the annoying trio was still watching him. He shot all three a dirty look then pulled the phone closer to his face. "Hey. What's up?"

"Is this a bad time?"

"No." He frowned at his rapt audience then shifted, wedging himself as close to the window as he could. His eyes moved back to the screen, focusing on Courtney. Her face was drawn, tired, maybe a little pale. Wisps of hair floated around her face, like she'd been running her hands through it over and over—or maybe trying to pull it out. "Everything okay? Is something wrong?"

"Your son is what's wrong."

A thrill shot through him at words. *Your son.* Would he ever get tired of hearing that? Ever stop feeling that warm sense of pride? Christ, he hoped not.

Then the rest of the words sunk in and he frowned. "What happened? Is everything okay? Isn't he sleeping?"

"He's having a meltdown. I've never seen him act this way. Usually I can get him to calm down but..." Her voice trailed off but not before he heard the desperation in it. He pulled the phone closer, saw the almost frantic light in her eyes.

"Is he sick? Does he have a fever?"

"No. I thought so too at first but no, it's not that." She glanced over her shoulder then looked back at him. "This is just a full-blown meltdown. I thought...would you talk to him? Maybe if he saw you—"

"Yeah." Harland cleared his throat, trying to dislodge the unexpected lump. "Yeah, sure."

Relief crossed her face a second before it disappeared from the screen. He watched as the background changed, caught a glimpse of the hallway floor, the edge of a door, the carpeting on the floor of Noah's room.

Then he saw his son's face, angry and tear-streaked, red and blotchy. He was crying, screaming his version of displeasure. And whoa, okay. Harland had never seen him quite like this before. Meltdown? Yeah, that was one way to describe it.

The background changed again, whirring across the screen. Courtney had picked Noah up, was trying to juggle his squirming son and the phone at the same time. Then all he saw was the floor as she started walking. She must be going into her room, or someplace where she could sit the phone down to hold Noah and talk and sign all at the same time. He sure as hell hoped so.

He looked up, saw three sets of eyes on him. Watching, listening. "Come on guys, really? Can you maybe mind your own fucking business?"

"I heard that."

Harland jumped, looked back at the screen. Courtney was watching him, one eyebrow raised, a hint of a smile tugging at one corner of her mouth. But she still looked frazzled, tired, at wit's end.

"Uh, sorry."

The background moved as she placed the phone on the makeshift stand on her dresser. Then she shifted and Noah appeared on the screen with her. He was still crying, his back arching as he swung his arms, the stuffed plane clutched in one fist.

Courtney snapped her fingers in front of him, trying to get his attention. Once, twice. "Noah. Noah, look who it is. See? Look who it is."

She pointed at the phone—at Harland—then snapped her fingers again. "Noah, sweetie. Look. It's Daddy. See? There's Daddy."

Harland froze, unable to move, to blink, to breathe. Courtney snapped her fingers again, finally got Noah's attention, then made a sign for him: her hand held straight out, fingers spread wide, thumb tapping against her forehead.

Father.

Daddy.

"See Noah? It's Daddy. Daddy's right here. Look."

Noah quieted down, his eyes watching Courtney as she made the sign over and over again. He hiccupped, shook his head, hiccupped again then finally looked over at the phone.

Harland bit the inside of his cheek, hard, trying to not lose it. He couldn't lose it, not here, not now. But how could he not? His son was watching him, a smile on his face, his hand making the sign for *Daddy*.

Noah was calling him Daddy.

Harland pulled air into his lungs, trying to fill them before he passed out. His eyes burned, felt gritty and tired, and he made a quick swipe at them with a hand that shook too much. Then he smiled, almost laughed.

"Hey little man. It's okay. Daddy's here." Harland's free hand unclenched and he brought it up, hesitant at first, almost awkward as he made the sign. Again, more comfortable this time. "Daddy's here. So stop giving Mommy a hard time, okay?"

Noah's grin grew wider and he reached for the phone, the screen filling with his tiny hand. He heard Courtney in the background saying something, saw the two of them reappear on the screen as she pulled Noah away. He looked at his mom, bounced up and down in her arms, then pointed at the screen and made the sign for *Daddy* again.

"Yes, you little monster. Just like I told you." She dropped a kiss on the top of his head then looked back at Harland. "He kept asking for you, wouldn't settle down. I didn't know what else to do."

"Uh, yeah." Harland cleared his throat, had to stop himself from rubbing his eyes again. "No problem. So, uh—that's a new one, huh?"

He didn't have to explain what he meant and Courtney didn't even pretend to misunderstand. She offered him a small smile, so tender. A softness filled her eyes, releasing some of the stress and tension that had been there when she first called.

"We've been working on it. It, uh, it didn't take him long to pick it up."

Harland nodded, tried to swallow around the lump in his throat, blinked against the burning in his eyes. He tried to talk, had to stop and clear his throat. "Thank you."

Courtney's tender smile grew wider and she nodded. She bent down, picked up the stuffed plane Noah had dropped, then moved closer to the phone. "Say goodnight to Daddy, Noah."

His son leaned in, sleepiness already dancing across his tired face, and waved goodnight. He pulled the plane against his chest, let his head drop to his mother's shoulder.

"Goodnight, little man." Harland made a quick sign then hesitated. Slowly, each movement careful and deliberate, he made a second one.

Courtney watched him for a long second, her face carefully blank. "That's, uh, that's not the sign for 'plane'."

He captured her gaze, held it, gave her a small smile. "I know." Then he disconnected the call before she could say anything, before he could see her reaction.

He jammed the phone back into his pocket and took a deep breath, ready to fend off the teasing he was sure he'd get. But nobody was watching him, nobody was paying attention to him. In fact, the terrible trio was nowhere to be found. When had they moved to give him privacy? He didn't know, didn't care.

He settled back in the seat and stretched his legs out, getting as comfortable as he could. Then he closed his eyes, a smile on his face as he replayed the video call over and over in his mind.

Daddy.

CHAPTER TWENTY-TWO

Harland wiped his sweaty palm on his pants then tried to get the key into the lock one more time without it slipping through his hand. Why the fuck was he so nervous? He shouldn't be.

He glanced over his shoulder, tried to smile at Courtney, then turned back. Yeah, he was fucking this up, he could tell by the odd little look she had given him. He took a deep breath, finally got the key to turn, and pushed open the door.

He palmed the switch and moved to the side, letting her in. This was only the second time she had been here—unless you counted that morning a few weeks ago, which he didn't. He didn't even like to think about that morning. And he didn't count the first time she had been here, either, because it had been too formal, too stiff. Too confrontational.

This time was about them, just the two of them.

She stepped inside, shrugging out of her coat as she looked around. Her face was carefully blank, her eyes revealing nothing of what she thought.

Harland tossed the keys on the small table by the door

then jammed his hands into his back pockets. What did she think? What did she see when she looked around?

Probably the same thing he saw: a bare bones bachelor pad in desperate need of a talented decorator. Or even an untalented one. It was livable, even comfortable, he'd admit that much.

It had the requisite sofa and chairs, large television and audio system. Coffee table, end tables, lamps. But that was about it. His place was missing that welcoming lived-in feel he got whenever he was at Courtney's. Her place was a home. This...this was just a place to crash.

"I, uh, I had a cleaning company come in. To get rid of the cigarette smoke and shit. You can't still smell it, can you?"

Courtney shook her head, gave him a small smile. "It smells fine."

"Okay, good. I was worried—I told him not to smoke in here but..." Harland's voice trailed off. Why the fuck was he even bringing up his father? He gave himself a mental shake and moved toward the living room, stopping before he got to the small hallway leading to the large eat-in kitchen—and the bedrooms in the back.

"Did you, uh, want the quick tour?"

"Sure." It looked like she was trying to hide her smile and Harland couldn't figure out why. Was she humoring him? Or did he look as uncomfortable as he felt?

"So. This is the kitchen. Like you couldn't figure that out, right?" He laughed, the sound a little forced, and waved his hand around. Yeah, it was definitely a kitchen, with a refrigerator and stove and dishwasher and cabinets. It even had a table with four chairs, in case she wasn't sure it was an eat-in kitchen.

Yeah, because it was so hard to tell.

Harland gave himself a mental shake and moved down the hallway, pointing as he went. "Bathroom. Spare bedroom that I use for an office." He pointed out the desk and computer, the overstuffed chair that probably needed replacing. "The other spare bedroom. It's, uh, empty now. And, uh, the master bedroom is through there."

No way was he going to take her in there. He didn't want her to get the wrong idea, even it was really the *right* idea because that's all he could think of. He just didn't want *her* to know that.

Although she probably did, because she gave him a small nod and looked away—but not before he saw her smile. And yeah, he was being an ass. There was no reason for him to be this uncomfortable, none at all. It wasn't like this was their first date or anything.

Except it was. Kind of. They hadn't gone anywhere by themselves since the day he'd learned about Noah. Hell, they hadn't really gone anywhere, period. They'd gone out for dinner after that one hockey game, gone to family skate. That was pretty much it.

So he wanted tonight to be...if not *special*, at least nice. He just wasn't sure how to make that happen.

Courtney headed back toward the kitchen, still looking around, taking things in. Then she turned the corner and disappeared from his view. Getting something to drink? Yeah, probably. He heard the refrigerator open, heard her moving things around.

He followed her, leaning against the doorframe and just watching her. A bottle of white wine was in one hand as she used the other to open and close drawers—probably searching for a corkscrew.

"Top drawer over to your left."

She glanced over her shoulder, gave him a smile. "Thanks."

"Yeah. I babyproofed it."

Courtney paused, her hand reaching into the drawer. Then she looked over her shoulder once more, frowning. "You babyproofed the corkscrew?"

"What? No. This place. I babyproofed it. Well, I tried to. Uh, in case Noah ever comes over and...well, in case he comes over." He took a deep breath, trying to figure out what that look on Courtney's face meant. Should he tell her what else he was thinking of doing? What he wanted to do? Probably not. But his mouth had a mind of its own and decided to keep on talking.

"I was thinking we could go shopping this week and maybe, you know, buy some kid furniture and shit so Noah has...a place..." His voice drifted off, his mouth finally coming to the same conclusion his mind had already made. Courtney was staring at him, her mouth slightly open, surprise in her eyes—and not exactly the kind he had hoped to see.

"Harland, I don't think—"

"Never mind. Stupid idea." Did his face look as hot as it felt? Probably. He forced a smile and pushed away from the doorframe, reached around her to grab the corkscrew. He took the bottle from her hand and nodded toward one of the cabinets. "Glasses are in there. I'll get this."

"Harland—"

"No, it's okay. Really." He stepped to the side, turning slightly so she couldn't see him. And fuck, now his damn hands were shaking. Stupid. So fucking stupid.

He finally got the fucking bottle opened. He tossed the cork—still attached to the corkscrew—to the side and turned, expecting Courtney to hand him a glass so he could fill it. She hadn't moved, hadn't bothered to even look for the glasses. He looked at her, saw that same expression in her eyes, and looked away. Fine, he'd get the glasses himself, find some way to change the subject.

She placed her hand on his arm, stopping in. But he still wouldn't look at her. He couldn't.

"Harland." She took a deep breath, let it out on a heavy sigh. "We need to talk."

"No, we're good. I told you, forget I said anything. Stupid idea."

"I didn't mean—"

"Courtney. Stop. I said it was cool. Let it go." He shrugged off her hand and moved past her, grabbed two glasses from the cabinet. He placed both on the counter, filled them, put the bottle to the side. Then he grabbed his own glass and headed to the living room.

And he managed to do it without stomping—too much.

He sat in the middle of the sofa, took a long swallow of the wine. Why the fuck was he even drinking this? He wasn't a wine drinker, never had been. But isn't that what people drank when they were having a romantic night? Yeah, sure. At least it wasn't red. He couldn't—wouldn't—drink red wine. Couldn't even stand the smell of it.

He took another swallow, grimaced, and placed the glass on the table. Then he leaned forward and dropped his head into his hands, trying not to think.

How could he *not* think? He had hoped this would be a nice romantic night for them. A real date. They'd gone out to dinner. Talked, laughed. Just the two of them. Then he brought her back here because her mother had been adamant when she told them not to worry about coming home early—or at all.

Yeah, he'd brought her back here and completely ruined everything by running his fucking mouth.

He heard Courtney's hesitant steps, felt the sofa dip as she took a seat next to him. Then she wrapped her hand around his arm, rested her head against his shoulder, and sighed.

"I'm sorry. You freaked me out a little."

He tried to shrug, couldn't because he was worried she'd move if he did. "Don't worry about it."

"Don't you want to know why?"

Fuck no, he didn't want to know. He didn't think he could handle whatever her reason would be. "No. I'm good."

She was quiet for a long time, long enough that he thought now would be a safe time to change the subject. But as soon as he shifted, as soon as he opened his mouth, Courtney started talking.

"I'm still getting used to all of this. Used to you being around. It's...for the longest time, it's just been me and mom in Noah's life. And when you said you wanted to buy kid furniture, I got scared."

Harland tilted his head, watching her. She chewed on her lower lip, not quite looking at him. He leaned back, wrapped his arm around her and pulled her closer. "Why would that scare you?"

"Why? Because I'm not used to sharing him. I'm not used to anyone else being in his life. This is all happening so fast." She glanced at him, looked away and brushed the hair out of her face. "And because it's going to take some time getting used to letting him sleep over here."

What was she saying? Harland repeated the words to himself, his scowl deepening each time. "Is that what you thought? Courtney, I didn't mean for him to visit, to sleep over. I mean, I did, but not the way you're thinking. I meant—"

She kept watching him but he couldn't tell what she was thinking. Could he tell her why? Could he go through with asking her to move in? He wanted to. He wanted that more than anything: for them to be a family. To be together. He wanted to come home and have her face be the first he saw when he walked through the door. Wanted Noah to run up to him with his bright smile, wanted to scoop him up and toss him in the air and kiss his wife and—

Whoa. Holy fuck. Where the hell had that come from? *Wife?* No. No, that was *not* what he'd been thinking. He was going to ask her to move in. That was it. Just...move in. He wasn't ready for marriage. He didn't think she was ready, either. There was still too much between them, too much shit from their past to work out.

Wasn't there?

He didn't know. Fuck, he didn't know anything anymore. But the more the idea played in his head, the more right it felt. They were his family. Courtney had always been his family, from the very first moment he laid eyes on her all those years ago.

He looked back at her, the words on the tip of his tongue, fighting to come out. He took a deep breath, opened his mouth...closed it again. He couldn't do it. Not yet, not when she was looking at him like she was expecting the worst.

"I, uh, I just meant he should have a place to sleep. You know, in case...in case you guys wanted to spend the night. That was all." The words fell flat but there was nothing he could do about that now. And she was still looking at him, that odd expression in her eyes. A cross between disappointment and shock and...he couldn't tell what.

He leaned forward, reached for the glass of wine and drained it one swallow. For the first time in a long time, he couldn't tell what Courtney was thinking, couldn't *feel* what she was feeling. That bothered him, for reasons he couldn't quite put into words.

It didn't help that Courtney laughed, the clear sound filled with something that almost sounded like relief. "Sorry. I guess I just jumped to the wrong conclusion. I'm off on Thursday. We could go shopping then. If you want."

"Yeah, sure. I can pick you up after practice." He leaned back, forced a smile he didn't quite feel. He needed to get over this. Did he really want to ruin the rest of the night, thinking of everything he had wanted to say but was too fucking scared to? No, he didn't. This night was supposed to be just for them. The two of them. By themselves.

He leaned to the side and wrapped his arm around Courtney, planning on pulling her closer. But instead of meeting him for a kiss, like he'd expected, she rested her head against his shoulder and gave him a tiny smile.

"Is practice going any better?"

No. "About the same."

"Still not able to score?"

Fuck no. And he was starting to think he'd have the same problem tonight. "Not yet, no."

"You shouldn't worry about it too much. I'm sure it'll happen soon enough."

Christ he hoped so. "Tyler said I was trying too hard."

"Maybe."

No, no *maybe* about it. He hadn't even started trying yet. "Jason said I was jinxed. Zach said I was cursed."

"Why would they say something like that?"

Because they were both assholes. "Who knows? Jason thinks it has something to do with why my game went to shit last year but it doesn't. Not even close."

Courtney shifted, pressing closer as she looked up at him. "What did happen last year? You still haven't told me."

And fuck, why had he brought that up? He hadn't meant to, hadn't even realized they were skirting that close to the subject. "Nothing. I don't want to talk about it."

He felt her stiffen beside him, felt her start to pull away. Yeah, there was no missing the disappointment in her eyes. She opened her mouth, ready to say something, but he didn't want to hear it, was afraid she'd somehow talk him into telling her. And no way in hell was he going to do that.

So he leaned forward and captured her mouth with his. She stiffened under his touch and for a horrifying second, he was afraid he fucked up again, that she knew he was trying to distract her. Yeah, she knew. Courtney knew him better than he knew himself.

But she didn't pull away, didn't push him away. Her arms slid around his neck and she moved closer, like she was trying to climb inside him. Her mouth opened under his, her tongue sweeping out to meet his.

And he was lost. Completely, totally lost. How could it still be this way between them? After everything they'd been through. After everything that had happened. He didn't want to question it, didn't want to think about it. He just wanted to feel it.

He twisted, got his arm under her legs, and stood, holding her against him. She tightened her arms around his neck and pulled back, her eyes already glazed with the same passion that seared him.

"Bedroom. *Real* bed." His voice was husky, low and thick, but she understood the words, gave him a small seductive smile that damn near made him drop her. He made it back to the bedroom, yanked the covers back with one hand then lowered her to the mattress. He stretched out beside her, his leg trapping hers as he captured her mouth once more.

She tasted like heaven, sweet and spicy. She tasted like home, warm and comforting. He deepened the kiss, claiming and possessing even as he lost a little bit more of himself. He dragged his hand along her side, grabbed the hem of her shirt and slid it up. Skin, soft and flush, its warm smoothness so different from his own.

Harland broke the kiss, pushed himself over her so he was straddling her, and skimmed his hands along her sides, moving the sweater up. Slow, so slow, like a present to be savored.

Too slow.

Courtney pulled her arms from the sleeves, yanked the sweater over her head then reached for the buttons on his shirt. He grabbed her wrists and held them above her head, pinning her in place.

"Not yet." He dropped a kiss against her mouth, dragged his lips along her neck. Gently nipped at the muscle between her neck and shoulder, sucked at the skin until he heard her gasp, felt her hands tighten around his.

He kissed her again, released his hold on her wrists and ran the tip of one finger from her chin, down her throat, lower. Slow, so slow. Down to her cleavage, across the swell of soft flesh pushing against the lacy cups of her bra.

He watched her, waited for her eyes to flutter open.

Then he grinned. "Don't move. No matter what I do, don't move your arms."

She opened her mouth to say something, probably to tell him no. Or ask him why. He shook his head in silent warning and ran his thumbnail across the hard peak of one nipple. She gasped, closed her eyes as her head fell back.

"Don't move."

He watched as her fingers dug into the mattress above her head. But she didn't move. Harland smiled then kissed his way down her body, pulled a hard nipple between his teeth, sucked it through the smooth lace. She shifted under him, her hips surging up, reaching.

Harland tightened his legs around her thighs, using his weight to press her against the mattress. He ran his tongue along the swell of her breast, used one hand to pinch and tease her nipples. Kissing, sucking, licking. Always through the lace, the rasp of material rough against his tongue.

Rough against her skin.

She moaned, soft little sighs that shot through him, made his cock strain against his pants. He shifted again, moving lower, then grabbed the lacy edge of her bra and pulled it down over her breasts.

He cupped her soft flesh, squeezing, his thumbs circling each nipple. Soft, hard. Slow, fast. Over and over as she tried to move beneath him. He dipped his head, ran his tongue between her breasts, moved his head and captured a hard nipple between his teeth again. He bit down, used a gentle suction to pull the hard peak into his mouth, capturing it between his tongue and the roof of his mouth.

Courtney gasped again, a high-pitched moan. Her back arched and her fingers dug deep into the mattress. But she didn't reach for him, not yet.

He slid down her legs, his fingers making quick work of the snap and zipper of her jeans. He dragged them down to her thighs, trapping her legs so she couldn't move them, couldn't spread them. Then he straddled her again, his legs tight around hers. Leaned forward, dragged the tip of his finger across her stomach, down along her hip bone, following the edge of the matching lacy underwear. She moaned, tossed her head from side to side, tried to raise her hips.

Harland watched her, his eyes burning with fever at each little move, at each tiny sound. He dipped his finger under the edge of her underwear, across the heat of her soft flesh. Back out, across to the other side. Back and forth, his touch gentle, teasing.

She was panting now, her chest rising and falling with each harsh breath, her nipples hard, erect. His cock strained against his jeans, almost painful, eager for release. He ran a hand along his hardened length, closed his eyes and bit back a groan.

No, not yet.

He grabbed her hips, lowered his head and licked her through the lace. He could taste her even then, sweet and salty, a delicacy only he had savored. "I love the way you taste."

Her only reply was a soft moan, a harsh breath as he licked her again. He dipped his thumbs into the lacy waistband, pulled the underwear past her hips. Dragged his thumb across her soft folds, back and forth.

He leaned forward, used his other hand to separate her flesh. Ran his nail down along her clit. Gently at first, then harder. Watching her hips tilt toward his touch, watching as her body sought more. Her legs trembled under him, the muscles of her thighs tightening as she tried to spread them, tried to open herself to more of his touch.

He dipped his head, ran his tongue along the hard flesh of her clit. Pulled it between his teeth, sucked and licked. Her back arched again, her moan a desperate gasp. Part pleasure, part pain.

He slid a finger into her, felt her muscles clench around him. Slid it out, heard her sigh. In, out. He stroked her with his tongue, harder, his finger mimicking the rhythm.

"Harland." She called his name, her voice hoarse, pleading. "Harland, p-please."

He raised his hand, watching her through half-closed eyes, his finger still stroking her. "Tell me what you want."

"Y-you. Always...you." She arched her back, her hips rolling under his. Seeking, demanding. "You're all I've ever wanted."

Her body shook as her climax swept over her. A flush crept across her skin, her chest heaved with each harsh breath as she cried his name.

Harland reached for his jeans, popped the button with clumsy fingers. Fuck. He'd wanted to play, wanted her to feel just a fraction of what he felt when he was with her, inside her.

It had backfired on him.

He jumped off the bed, kicked off his pants as he dragged hers down her legs. Then he was covering her body with his, his arms tight around her as he captured her mouth...

And plunged deep inside her.

She wrapped her legs high around his waist, pulling him in deeper. Her hands stroked his body, her nails digging into his back as he drove into her. Harder. Deeper.

"Tell me again." He kissed her, pulled back. "Tell me."

"You. I want you." Her head fell back, her body arched as she climaxed again. Her inner muscles tightened, clenching, over and over until he became part of her.

He'd always been part of her.

He captured her face between his hands, kissed her, deep and possessive as he drove into her. His hips pumped, faster, a desperation he didn't understand consuming him.

And then his climax shattered around him. His vision went dark, slowly filled with pinpricks of light. Reds and oranges and whites, each explosion matching the pounding of his heart. He slowed the kiss, pulled away, worried that he might have somehow hurt Courtney, that he'd been too rough, too hard.

He sucked in a lungful of air, forced his eyes open, saw Courtney staring up at him. Her warm eyes were glazed with passion...and with the same wonder he felt dancing in his chest.

He smiled, leaned down for a quick kiss, pulled back just the tiniest bit. "I love you."

She reached for him, dragged the tip of her finger along his lower lip, the touch gentle, reassuring. "I know."

CHAPTER TWENTY-THREE

"You need your head examined."

Courtney blew the hair from her eyes and kept walking. Maybe if she ignored Beth enough, she'd stop talking. Or if she walked faster, Beth would just give up and find some place to sit and wait for her instead of harping on her.

This was her fault. What had she expected when she asked Beth to go shopping with her? It was supposed to be nothing more than a leisurely few hours at the mall. Try on some clothes, maybe get a free makeover at the department store's cosmetic counter. Splurge on a giant gourmet pretzel when they were done.

Yeah, that's what it *should* have been—until Courtney opened her big fat mouth. She should have known better, should have just kept her mouth shut. But she needed to talk to someone—someone besides her mother, who made it quite clear that she thought she was insane.

Maybe her mom and Beth could move in together, since they both thought the same thing.

"Would you stop running? My legs aren't as long as yours!"

Courtney blew out an impatient sigh and stopped,

waited for Beth to catch up to her. "I wasn't running."

"You were walking fast. That's the same thing as running as far as I'm concerned." Beth looked around, frowning at the harried shoppers passing around them. Then she rolled her eyes and grabbed Courtney's arm, dragging her over to an empty bench out of harm's way.

"Sit." She pushed Courtney to the bench then stood in front of her, hands on her hips. What was she going to do? Tackle Courtney if she decided to get up? Probably.

She crossed her arms in front of her and scowled at her former best friend. "Fine. I'm sitting."

"Good." Beth just stood there, hands still on her hips, staring. And she kept staring.

"What?"

"Start talking."

"No." Courtney tried to stand, only to have Beth push her back down.

"Out with it. Tell me what's really going on."

"I told you."

"No, you didn't. Your *words* said you thought you were seeing too much of Harland and that you thought maybe you should back it off some. As in, all the way. Your *eyes* said the whole idea of doing that scared the living shit out of you. And *I* think you're totally bat shit crazy for even saying something like that because you're totally in love with him."

"I am—"

"Oh, don't even say it. You are, too, and I don't know who the hell you're trying to convince otherwise. Now out with it: what happened?"

"Nothing happened. It's just—everything. Everything happened."

"Yeah, you're definitely in love. You even sound insane."

"I'm not—"

"Oh my God. Yes, you are. In love *and* insane. Stop denying it. Now tell me what happened."

Courtney flopped back against the bench, clenching her jaw. If she had a bag nearby, she'd probably punch it. Or kick it. But she didn't, because she hadn't bought anything. She didn't *want* to buy anything, she just wanted to get away from everything for a few hours, away from her mixed emotions and whirling thoughts.

Except she couldn't, not when she was the one who had made the mistake of bringing everything up in the first place.

Beth made a screeching sound, startling her. Her friend rolled her eyes, ran both hands through her hair until it stood up in every direction. Then she plopped down next to Courtney and leaned in close, like she was trying to be threatening.

"Tell. Me. What. Happened." She said the words through clenched teeth, reminding Courtney of an angry beaver—not exactly the most complimentary comparison. She bit back a laugh that came dangerously close to ending in a sob.

"He said he loved me."

Beth pulled back like she'd just been slapped. "Okay. And this is a bad thing, why?"

"Because everything has happened too fast. Because he's hiding something from me. And if he's hiding something from me, how can I be sure he's telling the truth?"

"Too fast? Um, correct me if I'm wrong, but haven't you guys known each other forever?"

"Yeah. Fourteen years."

"Fourteen years? Whoa. Holy shit. Really? That long? That's...wow. No kidding?"

Courtney nodded. What else could she say? It *was* a long time.

"Okay, so you've known him practically your whole life. Not to mention the fact that he's Noah's father so it's not like you guys don't have a romantic history..." Beth's voice drifted off as her eyes lost their focus, like she was suddenly somewhere else. Courtney looked around, wondering if maybe Beth had seen someone she knew—or someone she wished she knew.

Then her hand dashed out and gripped Courtney's arm, started lifting it up and down in some kind of crazy wave. "Oh. My. God. No way. Tell me no way."

Courtney pulled her arm free and slid back two inches to put more distance between them. "Okay. No way."

Beth screeched, reached for her arm again, only this time, Courtney was faster. Beth frowned, like she'd just been denied a prize, then screeched again.

"Harland's the only guy you've had sex with, isn't he?"

"Keep your voice down!" Courtney glanced around, looking to see if anyone had overheard her. One or two people looked their way then kept walking. Courtney slid down in the seat, trying to hide.

"Oh my God. It's true. You've never been with anyone else! I can't believe it. Well, yes I can but still—wow. No way."

"Stop it. People are starting to look this way."

"They are not. You're just paranoid. And who cares if they are? I think it's sweet. So what—did he ruin you for other men? Is that it? I've seen pictures of him and he has huge hands and you know what they say about the size of a man's hands and—"

Courtney slapped her hand over Beth's mouth, stopping her before she could say anything else. "Enough. Just—stop."

Beth mumbled something and narrowed her eyes. Courtney narrowed her own eyes in response. "If I move my hand, promise you'll shut up?"

Beth glared, then finally nodded. Courtney moved her hand, but only a few inches, waiting. When her friend remained quiet, she finally lowered her hand to her lap.

"Is it true? What they say about a man's hands?"

"That's it. I'm done." Courtney pushed off the bench, prepared to leave Beth behind. But Beth had other ideas and pulled her back.

"Okay, okay. I'm sorry. I'll stop. It's just—that's not something you hear every day, you know? I think it's sweet." Beth paused, tilted her head to the side. "Do you think he—"

Courtney shot her a look that must have been more threatening than she realized because Beth shut up immediately.

"Okay, guess not. Of course not. Men are pigs. Death to all men. Who needs them? You're right. Dump his ass. The pig."

"Beth! Can you be serious for just one minute? I don't want to 'dump him'."

"Ha! I knew it!"

Courtney ignored her and kept on talking. "I just think...I think we need to take a break. Just for a little while." And God, just the words were enough to bring tears to her eyes. She didn't *want* to take a break. But she was so afraid they were moving too fast. And she *knew* he wasn't being completely honest with her. That bothered her most of all. Something had happened last year. Even his teammates knew that. So why couldn't he tell her what it was? And if he was hiding that, what else was he hiding?

"Courtney, you're my best friend and I love you like a sister, but I think you'd be making the biggest mistake of your life if you walked away from him." Beth leaned closer, placed her hand on Courtney's arm and squeezed. She wasn't used to seeing Beth this serious and almost wished she'd go back to making inappropriate comments. The serious Beth scared her.

No—it was what she was saying that scared her. Because she was afraid Beth was right.

"My mother said the same thing."

"Then that's two out of three of us. Don't you think that maybe we're right? I mean, I know you guys went through some shit and all, but damn—you've known him your whole life. He's Noah's father. And I see the way you look when you talk about him."

"Yeah? Like what? Scared?"

"Maybe. But also like someone in love. And don't say you don't love him because I know you do. I don't think you've ever stopped."

"Okay. So I love him. I always have. But I'm so afraid that there's something else going on, something he doesn't want to share. And after what happened last time, I'm afraid…"

"Afraid of what?"

Courtney took a deep breath and let it out in a rush. She ran her finger along her leg, her nail scraping at the frayed edge of the hole by her knee. "Last time, right before things ended, I knew something was going on with him. I could *feel* it. And I kept asking him but he wouldn't tell me. And then everything blew up and he just…left. If he had told me what was going on, if he had trusted me enough to tell me what his father was saying and doing, we could have talked about it and maybe things would have never ended. I'm just afraid of the same thing happening again, only this time, I have Noah to worry about."

"Have you tried to talk to him?"

"Yeah."

"Like how?"

"What do you mean, like how?"

"Just what I said. Did you tell him what you just told me?"

"No. I just asked him what happened."

"That was it? Nothing else?"

"No. I didn't think—"

"You know, for as smart as you are, sometimes you can be really stupid. You need to talk to him. Like, really talk to him. Tell him what you told me. And then give him time to tell you what happened. Maybe he's not ready to talk about it yet, you know? But you can't just go assuming the worst without talking to him."

"I don't know. Maybe—"

"No 'maybe' about it." Beth stood, grabbed Courtney's hand and pulled her to her feet. "When are you supposed to see him again?"

"Tomorrow morning. I'm taking Noah to watch him practice. And then we're supposed to go to the game tomorrow night."

Beth lopped an arm through hers and started walking, practically dragging Courtney along. "Perfect. Good thing I have off tomorrow."

"Why is that a good thing?"

"Because I'm going to practice with you. I want to meet this guy. Besides, you need to know someone will be there to kick your ass if you chicken out."

"Beth, I don't think that's a good idea."

"Sure it is. Now come on, we have plans to make. Or rather, *I* have plans to make. You just need to listen."

CHAPTER TWENTY-FOUR

"For the love of...God damn son-of-a-bitch. You mother fucking, cock sucking piece of—hey, what the fuck?"

Harland spun around, ready to swing his stick at whatever stupid son-of-a-bitch had been brainless enough to clip him across the back of his leg. Aaron loomed over him, a scowl etched into his hard face.

"Cool it the fuck off, Day-glo. You're making an ass out of yourself." Aaron dipped his head to the side, toward the bench. Harland sucked in a deep breath and looked over, trying not to be obvious. Sure enough, the entire coaching staff was watching him. And the expression on Coach Torresi's face did not bode well. Fuck. Coach didn't have a scar running down his face that flashed red with warning like Sonny LeBlanc of the Banners did. He didn't need one, not with a face chiseled from marble and piercing green eyes that flashed like the devil's.

Harland was fucked. Truly, thoroughly fucked.

Was he trying too hard, like Tyler kept insisting? Or was he really jinxed, or cursed—or both—like Zach and Jason thought? What the fuck did it matter? He was in a dry spell. Fuck, it was more like a dry *vacuum*—and it was sucking his career right out from under him.

What sucked the most was that, other than scoring, the rest of his game was better than it had been in a long while. Nowhere near the top, not like his first few months with the Banners, but still good. And this morning had been going well. Smooth. He'd been sure, so fucking sure, that today would be the day. That the cloud would lift and the spell would be broken and that would be it. Hell, he'd *felt* it. That was how sure he'd been.

And then Courtney had shown up earlier than he'd expected, Noah toddling behind her. And she'd brought a friend. Okay, he hadn't expected that, but whatever. She smiled and waved, moved over next to the glass while her friend took Noah up to the stands.

He had time so he'd gone over to say hi, to steal a quick kiss. He'd been buoyed with optimism, ready to show off. Ready to finally get a damn puck into the fucking net.

And then she told him they needed to talk. Told him she was afraid he was hiding from her, afraid he was holding a piece of himself back.

How the fuck could she think that? He loved her! She knew he did. Although maybe that explained why she hadn't said it back, why she became too fucking quiet when he said it.

So what if she explained *why* she was afraid. And so what if part of him actually understood? He got it, he really did. He'd been wrong three years ago, hadn't stop to think. Maybe, just maybe, if he had talked to her back then, things would have worked out differently.

But maybe not. Because he'd been cocky, so full of himself, his focus on being the best. On thinking he was the best because he'd been called up by the Banners. Because he'd made the big time—or so he thought. Would he have listened to her? He didn't know.

But to say she was worried he was hiding from her? That she was afraid that maybe things were moving too fast? What the fuck?

No, she wasn't calling things off. She just wanted to let him know they needed to talk more about things. Later. When he had more time.

What the fuck did that even mean? What the fuck was he even supposed to make of that?

Harland released the death grip on his stick then ran his gloved hand across the back of his neck. He looked at the coaching staff again, saw that at least they had stopped staring at him. Then his eyes drifted up to the stands, where Courtney and Noah were sitting. Because yeah, of course they'd still be here.

Mother fucker.

He took a deep breath, let it out. Looked at Aaron. "How loud was I?"

"You weren't. Mostly just mumbling. But you were still acting like an ass. Anyone watching could see you were having a meltdown."

A meltdown. Great. Now he was acting just like Noah when he didn't get his way.

"I'm fucked, Aaron. I don't know what to do anymore. Nothing works. No matter what I do, what I try, nothing works. And I really thought—fuck. It doesn't matter. I'm done."

"Yeah, with that attitude, you are."

"Attitude has nothing to do with it. I mean, did you see the look Coach was giving me? I'm surprised the fucking ice didn't melt."

"You sure that wasn't just because of your little tantrum?"

"Yeah, pretty sure."

"I think you're just being paranoid."

"Yeah. Okay."

"Listen, you're having a dry spell. That's it. Everyone has them. Stop worrying about, stop getting so fucking tense. Lighten up. It'll happen."

"Not if Coach benches me."

"So your ice time sucks. You're preaching to the choir. I've been there, remember? Shit, I've been in worse slumps than you. Been bounced around, sent up, sent down. Moved all over the fucking place. The worse my attitude was, the worse my game became."

"What? So you think it's my attitude?"

"No. I think it *was* your attitude. And whatever the fuck happened to you last year. Come on, let's work on some passing so we don't get our asses chewed." Aaron pushed off, heading down ice with a puck. Harland followed him, his stick at the ready. Back and forth, easy passes, just warming up.

Harland kept his eyes away from the net, just in case. And he refused to look back into the stands.

"Your tensing again. I can see the way your stick twists to the right. Relax. Stop worrying about scoring. Remember why you started playing in the first place."

"What are you, a fucking life coach now?" Harland mumbled the words, didn't think they were loud enough for Aaron to hear until the other man laughed. He forced himself to relax. Deep breath in. Deep breath out. Deep breath in, deep breath out.

Tried to remember how it felt when he was kid, when all he wanted to do was lace up his skates and hit the ice. Pick up speed, faster and faster until he thought he'd fly. He never worried about the stick then, didn't have to. It was part of him, nothing more than an extension of his arm, his to command at will.

He closed his eyes, trying to recapture that feeling. His time on the ice had been the only time he'd truly been free. Away from his father, away from the insults and the random backhand because he happened to be standing in the wrong spot at the wrong time. He could be himself when he was on the ice, with nobody there to yell at him. He'd been accepted for who he was; nobody cared that his father was a loud bully, that his mother had walked out—

"Fuck!" Harland tightened his hands around the stick

as the puck careened past him. He forced himself to stay still, to not start swinging the stick in a childish fit. Why the hell had he thought about that? Now, of all times? He was trying to forget.

How could he forget, when that was the whole reason for his downward spiral?

"What the hell was that all about? You tensed up so bad, I could see it all the way over here."

"Nothing. It's—nothing." Harland shook his head, took off across the ice. Maybe if he did some laps, got rid of some of the tension...

Stopped fucking thinking about his mother. Why should he be thinking about her, when he barely remembered her? He'd been five when she just took off. He remembered her leaning over, giving him an absent pat on the cheek. Not a kiss, a fucking pat, like he was fucking dog or something. The scent of stale cigarettes and sweet red wine clung to her loose clothes, stuck in her platinum streaked hair. He remembered the sight of a faint bruise on her cheek, the slightly vacant expression in her glassy eyes.

She told him she had to leave. Told him she couldn't stay, couldn't take him with her no matter how much he cried. She didn't say goodbye, didn't try to console his tears. Just that quick pat on the cheek and a hollow 'I'll see you later'.

Only later never came.

And fuck. Fuck, fuck, fuck. Why? Why was he thinking about this? Now, of all times. He didn't need to be thinking about it, didn't want to remember it.

Except he never forgot.

He took another lap around the ice, gaining speed. Ignoring the whistle that signaled the end of practice, ignoring the looks he was getting from his teammates. Aaron, Zach, Jason, Tyler. All of them.

Fuck them. What did they know? He wanted it too much. He was too tense. He was cursed. He was jinxed.

He was all of the above.

He whirled past blurred faces, ignoring all of them as an odd calm closed over him.

He was all of the above.

One more lap, slower this time. The blurred faces became clearer as he passed them. Still watching him. He could see some of the expressions now, knew that they probably thought he'd completely lost his mind, that he'd come completely unhinged.

Except one. No, not one. Two.

One face wore nothing but a bright smile, wide honey-colored eyes dancing with delight. The other face wore an expression of concern, of worry, of silent understanding.

How the hell could she understand, when she didn't *know?* When nobody knew.

He was all of the above. He was his past. His present. But Courtney and Noah—they were his future. The only future that counted.

He slid to a stop, bent over with his stick across his knees and tried to catch his breath. He threw the stick across the ice, tossed his gloves to the ground. Reached up and undid the strap to his helmet, pushed it off his head and let it drop behind him. His stride was strong, purposeful, as he made his way to the door, unlatched it, stepped out onto the rubber flooring.

He could feel eyes on him, knew several of his teammates were watching. Probably the coaches, too. Fuck it. He didn't care. What were they going to do? Nothing worse than what he'd done to himself, what he'd allowed to happen.

He kept walking, his eyes focused on Courtney, only Courtney. She watched him, wariness crossing her face. Her arm tightened around Noah and she took a step back, bumped into a short woman who pushed her forward. Her friend. Harland didn't care, just kept advancing on her until he was less than a foot away.

Courtney tilted her head back, looking up at him with wide eyes. But she didn't try to step away again. And he saw it, in her eyes. Knew that she was expecting...something.

Harland cleared his throat, his voice strong and clear when he spoke. "My mother was a drunk. A convenient punching bag for my bully of a father."

"Harland—"

"She smelled like cigarettes and sweet wine. That's why I don't like red wine. Never have. She left when I was five. Patted me on the cheek, told me she'd see me later. Except she never did. She never came back."

Courtney blinked, reached out for him. He caught her hand, held it in his own. "Harland, you don't have to do this now. Not here."

"Yes, I do. I don't care who hears. The only things I care about are you and Noah." He squeezed her hand, tried to smile when she threaded her fingers with his. He took another deep breath, worried he wouldn't be able to find the words.

"I kept telling myself that if I was good enough, that if I could make the pros, then she'd come back. I convinced myself that nothing would stop me—because at some point growing up, I had convinced myself that she really *would* come back. Stupid, but there it is."

She squeezed his hand, gently encouraging him. Supporting him.

"I hired a private investigator. It took him a while, but he found her. Last year. And he contacted her, told her I was looking for her. She, uh—" He cleared his throat, couldn't understand why his vision was swimming. "She told him she wasn't interested. That she, uh, didn't want to see me. Didn't want me to contact her again."

"Oh God, Harland. I'm sorry. So sorry."

"After that, I just...stopped caring. Being the best didn't matter. It didn't matter if I screwed up or failed because succeeding didn't matter. Nothing mattered—until I came back here again and saw you. And Noah. Finding you again let me know that things do matter. Life matters."

Courtney's grip on his hand tightened, a reassuring connection that he needed more than he realized. She stepped forward and he pulled her into a hug, holding her close. Never wanting to let go. He dropped a kiss against her cheek, brushed his lips by her ear.

"I love you Courtney. I always have, from that first day I saw you on your porch, holding your doll and crying. I've never stopped loving you."

She pulled back, cupped his cheek with her hand. "I love you Harland. Now more than ever. I don't know what it's like *not* to love you and I don't want to know. Ever."

He tried to laugh but the sound came out strangled, hoarse. "Good, because I'm not going to let you. You're mine, Courtney. You and Noah. Always." He pressed a kiss against her lips, a quick one, no less powerful for its gentleness. Then he dropped a kiss on the top of Noah's head.

He looked down, saw Noah's face scrunch up as his tiny hand pushed against his chest. Then Noah peered up at him and grabbed his own nose and shook his head.

Harland blinked. Blinked again as a smile spread across his own face. The laughter built inside him, growing, expanding until it escaped in a clear strong sound, full of life, carrying away the dark weight he'd been wearing like an iron cloak. Courtney joined in, her own laughter light and musical as they stared at their son, watching as he told them, in no uncertain terms, that *Daddy stinks.*

CHAPTER TWENTY-FIVE

Harland swallowed back the disappointment in his gut as he looked at the giant screen suspended above center ice. They were halfway through the third period, up by two. But for him, the game was all but over.

Four minutes. That was all he'd been on the ice for this entire game. Four fucking minutes. Fuck, probably not even that long. He resisted the urge to glance behind him, to look at Coach Torresi. If he did, he might end up begging.

No, he wouldn't actually do that. He might *want* to but he wouldn't. He knew that this might happen, thought he had prepared himself for it.

He'd thought wrong.

He tightened his hands around the stick, twirled it back and forth. Left, right, back to the left. His foot kept bouncing, up and down, like he was keeping time to the fast beat of a song only he could hear. Nervous energy. A lot of it.

He took a deep breath, resigning himself, telling himself he'd get used to this. Maybe, if he said it enough, he really would. He just wished that he'd been able to talk

Courtney out of coming tonight. That's what made this whole thing worse: Courtney and Noah were in the stands, a few rows behind him, watching.

Or rather, not watching. At least, not watching him.

A shrill whistle split the air and Harland looked up, tried to clear his head and focus on what was happening on the ice. Play had been stopped in the offensive zone and there was some pushing and shoving going on. Travis Bankard skated back to the bench, a hand over his mouth, blood dripping from between his fingers. Coach Torresi leaned across the boards, pointing at the ref with the wad of rolled papers in his hands.

"You're not going to call that? Really? Look at him! That was high-sticking!" Coach shook his head, stepped back when one of the other coaches grabbed his arm to calm him down. Then he looked at Harland, those cold green eyes pinning him in place. Harland held his breath, waiting, trying not to hope.

"Day-glo."

"Sir?"

"You got that fucking monkey off your back now?"

Harland swallowed, nodded, knew his face was turning ten different shades of red. Yeah, he'd had an audience this morning. So what? He'd still do it again. "Yeah. Yes sir."

"We'll see. Now get your fucking ass out there and prove it."

Harland jumped the boards before Coach had finished talking, afraid he might change his mind. He hurried over, got into position. Aaron glanced over at him, gave him a quick nod.

The puck dropped and Aaron fought for possession, got the edge of it and passed it behind him, shooting it between his legs toward Jason. Harland hustled backward, closer to the net, getting into position.

Not thinking, not feeling. Just trusting. Calling on instincts without questioning them.

Jason passed it back to Aaron. He skated in but didn't

have a clear shot. Harland watched as he pulled the stick back, was sure he'd take the shot anyway. A spot cleared in front of Harland and he moved in, ready for the rebound just in case.

Except Aaron didn't take the shot. His head jerked up, his gaze landing squarely on Harland a split second before passing the puck to him.

For a brief, horrifying second, Harland almost froze. Was convinced he would freeze, miss the puck, miss the shot. He pushed the fear away in the space of a rapid heartbeat.

No!

The puck hit the blade of his stick. He cradled it, smooth and gentle. Spun, got the edge of his blade under the puck, and sent it flying.

He froze, held his breath, watched as the puck soared through the air with a slowness that was agonizing.

Please. Please. Please.

He heard the soft whoosh, saw the net shift as the puck hit the back of it. Saw the red flight flashing and heard the roar of the horn.

It went in! Holy fuck, it went in!

He stood there for a brief second, wondering if maybe he imagined it. No, it was real. He'd scored. He'd finally fuckling scored.

He jumped up, raised his stick in the air, then spun in a jubilant circle, screaming as Aaron and Jason raced over to him to celebrate. He'd done it. He'd finally done it!

He headed back to the bench, saw Coach nod at him, telling him to stay out there. Harland stopped, knowing he probably looked like an ass with the broad smile on his face. He didn't care.

He looked up, his eyes scanning the seats behind the bench. His gaze found Courtney almost immediately. She was still standing, a smile almost as big as his on her face. His other half. His salvation. His soulmate.

Noah stood beside her, jumping up and down, clapping

his little hands. Did his son really understand what had just happened, or was he just celebrating because everyone else was? After all, he wasn't quite three yet, hadn't really been properly introduced to hockey.

Yet.

It didn't matter, that would be changing soon enough. Noah was his father's son, after all.

Courtney. Noah. His life. All he needed.

Harland nodded in their direction, then pulled one hand from his glove. He raised his arm, his hand palm out, his middle and ring fingers bent, the other fingers spread wide.

I love you.

EPILOGUE

Three Years Later

The seat belt jerked against Harland's shoulder. He reached for the dash, the console, anything he could grip, and shot a glare toward Jason. "Holy shit, would you slow the fuck down?"

"You just told me to speed up." Jason took the next corner, the wheels screeching against pavement. He grinned and cast a sideways glance at Harland. "You might want to change your shirt at least. We're not too far."

And risk doing a header through the windshield? Harland almost said no then changed his mind and unclipped the seat belt. "Just slow down enough so you don't get us killed."

"Relax. Everything will be fine." Jason took another corner, slamming Harland into the door.

Fine? Yeah, easy for him to say. But Harland just reached for the hem of the damp shirt, pulled it over his head and tossed it to the back seat. Grabbed the clean one from his bag and shrugged into it.

"It's inside out."

"Do I look like a give a fuck?"

"Guess not." One more turn, this one harder than before, and they were pulling into the main entrance. Jason hit the brakes, palmed the wheel to turn into the parking lot.

"No! Just drop me off at the front. You can park later."

"Whatever you say."

Harland didn't miss the laughter in Jason's voice, knew he was laughing at him. He wasn't overreacting, was he? No, no way. He glanced down, saw the way his hands were shaking. Okay, so maybe he was just a little nervous.

Jason slid to a stop at the front entrance. Harland grabbed his wallet off the dash and jumped out of the car, almost forgetting to shut the door until Jason called out to him. He spun around, slammed it, then took off at a run.

The receptionist at the lobby desk eyed him with an expression of amusement as he checked in, handed her his license and who knew what else that tumbled from his wallet. Did she have to be so damn slow? And he really wished she would stop smiling at him.

She finally returned his license—and everything else that had fallen from his wallet—along with a small plastic card. She was saying something, giving him instructions, but he didn't stop to listen, just took everything from her and hurried through the doors she was pointing at.

Calm down. Calm down.

How could he calm down? He couldn't. He hadn't been calm since receiving the phone call at practice a short while ago. He pushed his way around an elderly couple, barely managing to mutter an apology, then raced along the hallway to the elevators. And Christ, why were they so fucking slow? Didn't they know this was an emergency?

Okay, maybe not an emergency but still—he was in a hurry. He'd never forgive himself if he missed this. Hell, Courtney wouldn't forgive him.

He got off at the third floor, turned left and raced to the double doors, tried pulling on them.

Locked.

Why the hell were they locked?

He noticed a card reader to the side of the doors, glanced at the plastic card the receptionist had given. That must have been what she was telling him—

He swiped the card, heard an electronic beep, grabbed the handle and pulled. Then he hurried down another hallway, his eyes searching for someone who looked like they knew what was going on. There, a nurse's station.

"I'm here. Where is she?"

Both nurses turned to look at him, the amusement on their faces similar to what he'd seen on the receptionist's downstairs. Why did everyone seem to find him so damn funny? This wasn't funny, not even close.

"Your name sir?"

Name. Name. Of course, they'd need his name. "Courtney. I mean, Harland. Day. My wife—she's supposed to be back here?"

The nurses exchanged a look he didn't even try to understand. The older one stood, her dark eyes raking him from head to toe, then nodded over her shoulder. "She's back in delivery. You can follow me. I, uh, I could probably find a pair of scrubs. If you'd like."

Harland almost ran her over, had to slide to a stop to avoid just doing that. "Scrubs?"

"Yes. At least the bottoms. You, uh, might be more comfortable."

What the hell was she talking about? Comfortable?

She smiled again and very pointedly lowered her gaze. Harland frowned, finally looked down to see what the hell was wrong.

His pants. How the fuck could he forget his fucking pants? He was standing there in the middle of the hallway, in the middle of labor and delivery, wearing nothing but an inside-out t-shirt, unlaced athletic shoes, oversized hockey socks…and compression shorts over his jockstrap.

He blinked, couldn't quite meet the woman's eyes as heat filled his face. "Uh, yeah. That might be a good idea."

"I wish I could have seen that."

"It wasn't funny."

"That's all the nurses have been talking about. You made quite an impression on them." Courtney watched as a deep flush filled Harland's face. He narrowed his eyes but didn't say anything. No, he was totally absorbed in the small bundle sleeping in his arms.

Charlene Joanna Day. Not even a full day old and she already had her father wrapped around her finger.

And her older brother, as well.

Courtney glanced down at Noah, ran a hand along his back as he snuggled against her, sleeping.

Her family. Together. Just as it should be.

"She's so beautiful." Harland raised his head, his gaze soft and tender as it met hers. "Just like her mother."

Warmth spread through Courtney at the love so clear in her husband's eyes, at the love washing over her. It had always been this way, from the first day they met.

No, that wasn't quite true. It was better. And it would keep getting better, every single day.

She reached out and took Harland's hands, threaded her fingers with his and squeezed. Could he feel it, the love she had for him? Yes, he could. Just like she could feel his love for her.

Never ending. Forever and ever.

Just the way it should be.

If you enjoyed *Playing The Game*, I hope you will leave a review. Even a short one helps other readers discover my books--and means so much to me! Thank you!

And be sure to sign up for my newsletter, *Kamps' Korner*, for exciting news, sneak peeks, exclusive content, and fun, games, and giveaways! You don't want to miss it!

Can't wait for the newsletter? Need to get your fix of hockey, firefighters, passion and news daily? Then please join me and a great group of readers and fans at *Kamps Korner on Facebook*!

PLAYING TO WIN
The York Bombers, Book 2

Jason Emory has one motto: play hard, love hard...and win at all costs. It doesn't matter if he's on the ice or playing the field, his only goal is to win. For a life goal, it sounds pretty good. So why does he feel like he's drifting aimlessly instead of having the world at his feet? At least, that's what it feels like until one hot night with a beautiful stranger who seems oddly familiar—a stranger he can't forget.

Megan Bradley loves working at her parents' bar. Why

shouldn't she, when that gives her a chance to see her long-time crush up close and personal? Not that Jason knows who she is, not when she's nothing more than a modern day ugly duckling swimming in a sea of glittering swans. At least, until her best friend hatches a plan for an extreme makeover.

All she wants is one night to never forget—but sometimes getting what you want isn't what you need. Can she walk away from the connection that should have never happened? And what happens when it's time to face the truth—especially when she realizes that one sexy hockey player will stop at nothing when it comes to winning?

PLAYING TO WIN
Available March, 2017!

ABOUT THE AUTHOR

Lisa B. Kamps is the author of the best-selling series *The Baltimore Banners*, featuring "hard-hitting, heart-melting hockey players" (USA Today), on and off the ice. Her *Firehouse Fourteen* series features hot and heroic firefighters who put more than their lives on the line and she's reintroducing a whole new team of hot hockey players in her newest series, *The York Bombers*.

In a previous life, she worked as a firefighter with the Baltimore County Fire Department then did a very brief (and not very successful) stint at bartending in east Baltimore, and finally served as the Director of Retail Operations for a busy Civil War non-profit.

Lisa currently lives in Maryland with her husband and two sons (who are mostly sorta-kinda out of the house), one very spoiled Border Collie, two cats with major attitude, several head of cattle, and entirely too many chickens to count. When she's not busy writing or chasing animals, she's cheering loudly for her favorite hockey team, the Washington Capitals--or going through withdrawal and waiting for October to roll back around!

Interested in reaching out to Lisa? She'd love to hear from you, and there are several ways to contact her:

Website:
www.LisaBKamps.com

Newsletter:
http://www.lisabkamps.com/signup/

Email:
LisaBKamps@gmail.com

Facebook:
https://www.facebook.com/authorLisaBKamps

Kamps Korner Facebook Group:
https://www.facebook.com/groups/1160217000707067/

Twitter:
https://twitter.com/LBKamps

Goodreads:
https://www.goodreads.com/LBKamps

Amazon Author Page:
http://www.amazon.com/author/lisabkamps

Instagram:
https://www.instagram.com/lbkamps/

BookBub:
https://www.bookbub.com/authors/lisa-b-kamps

Do you want to connect with a great group of hockey romance authors and like-minded hockey fans? Then please join me at The Sin Bin!

The Sin Bin is a fun place to talk to other hockey romance readers and hockey fans, discover new books you might enjoy, interact with romance authors, drool over the male physique, and to generally bask in the board-bashing, emotional, testosterone-filled world of hockey romance.

Made in the USA
Columbia, SC
17 October 2017